LUCIUS

AN ACQUISITION NOVEL

CELIA AARON

Lucius
Copyright © 2021
Celia Aaron

All rights reserved. This copy is intended for the original purchaser of this book only. No part of this book may be reproduced, scanned, or distributed in any printed or electronic form without prior written permission from Celia Aaron. Please do not participate in piracy of books or other creative works.

This e-book is a work of fiction. While reference may be made to actual historical events or existing locations, the names, characters, places and incidents are products of the author's imagination, and any resemblance to actual persons, living or dead, business establishments, events, or locales is entirely coincidental.

Cover: Mitchell Wick by LaneFotograf

Design: PerfectPear

LUCIUS

Lucius Vinemont ruined my life.

It was a long time ago. It feels like yesterday.

I haven't let it go, and I won't. Not until he's dead. Lucius is the bogeyman, the shadow under my bed, the nightmare that wakes me in my sleep.

I loved him once, in the foolish way of a teenage girl. Those feelings are buried deep, soaked in blood and covered in a fine ash. Because Lucius was never just a bad boy, he was so, so much worse.

When you shoot a man through the heart, he's supposed to die. But Lucius isn't a man. He's a monster. One who promises pleasures wrapped in pain.

But the closer I get to him, the more I realize he's not the only evil lurking in my past...

1

LUCIUS

A ghost flits through the forest at the southeastern edge of my property, the trees hiding its movements. But I can sense it even if I can't see it. It's been haunting me for weeks.

I sip my bourbon and kick my feet up on the second-floor balcony railing as a muggy nighttime breeze stirs and eddies around my home. Out there in the dark, someone is playing a game with me. One that will most likely end up with one of us dead. I flex my free hand, the knuckles scarred from a life of solving the "him or me" equation that has defined human existence since Cain and Abel. Unfortunately for the ghost, I always win, no matter the cost. This intruder will go down like the rest, but I'll wait for him to make his move. For now, it's enough to know he's out there as I lean back in my chair and breathe in the humid night.

The house's square edges and neat lines jut out into

the well-trimmed lawn, imposing its presence—my presence—on this piece of land. So different from what it once was. Gone is the gaudy French palace that once metastasized onto the dark Louisiana dirt. The overbearing estate and its master were both turned to ash five years before. But the Oakmont property has a special place in my past, so much so that I bought it and built my modern mansion on top of the former home's ruins. And if some of the victims' ashes are crushed beneath my feet with each step along my floors? All the better.

I take a bigger swallow of the bourbon, the burn nonexistent in this near-priceless bottle. Only the best for a Vinemont. I would laugh at the thought, but I'm too focused on the woods, the moonlight filtering through the leaves, the darkness holding sway, oozing around and between, coating the spaces where I can feel the ghost watching and waiting.

Enemies are nothing new. Not for a man like me. But I admit this one is different. Patient. Not coming for my blood in the sloppy, haphazard way that so many others have. This ghost is wary.

I raise my glass and tilt it a little. "To you, ghost." The liquor slides down easy, and I stand and return inside, the glass door sliding shut behind me with a near-silent thunk.

Heading down to the first floor, I bypass my main living area and delve even farther, descending the staircase into my damp basement. A small puddle glimmers, my reflection inky as I pass and make my way to the very back, the deepest and dankest spot in this part of Louisiana.

"How are we doing?" I pull a sparse chain on a bare bulb, the light immediate and bright.

A man squints at me, one eye swimming with blood and the other laboring beneath a black and swollen lid. "Let me out." His voice is quiet, hoarse from useless screaming.

"Not until you tell me what I want to know." I cross my arms over my chest. "I can wait, but I'm getting tired of coming to check on you. I have a business to run and shit to do."

"Fuck you." He strains against the barbed wire I've wrapped around him, but he isn't going anywhere. "My people will come for me. You can't keep me here without someone finding out. I'm a goddamn judge, for Chrissakes!"

"It's been three days, Leonard. Three days of you screaming and pissing yourself. No one has even sniffed around about you. Were you reported missing? Sure. Will anyone connect it to me? Not a fucking chance." I run a hand through my hair, a simple movement intended to calm the rage burning through my veins as I remember his sins. "You made a big mistake going after my nephew. The guys you sent died screaming. But first they squealed just like you're going to squeal."

The papery skin on his forehead wrinkles, and he

clenches his useless fists. "Someone will know. They're probably out there right now, waiting to storm this place. And once I'm free, they'll kill your filthy family—your brat nephew and nieces, their bitch of a mother, and your brothers. The Vinemonts will suffer for what they've done, the decent people they've murdered, the ruin they—"

"You tried to kill a child, Leonard." My calm voice belies the raging volcano inside me. "A six-year-old."

"A Vinemont," he spits.

"That was your mistake. Now, tell me who's behind it. I know you didn't come up with it on your own. That addled brain of yours isn't capable of any sort of real plan."

He stares up at me, malevolence in his battered eyes.

I've never been a patient man, and Leonard isn't doing a thing to change that. I want to twist his neck and hear it break, but I need to wait. And he's right—someone *is* out there watching me, but I have a gut feeling they aren't interested in this particular shitbag. Otherwise, the ghost would've materialized by now. No, the patient specter doesn't care for Leonard, likely doesn't even know he's here.

I try a new tack, one that's never worked for me before. "Give me names, and I'll let you off with a warning. I'm a reasonable man."

"I know what kind of man you are, Lucius." He

spits a bloody wad of snot onto the wet floor, sending ripples through the swamp water.

That's too bad, because if he's telling the truth—if he has any real inkling of what I'm capable of—he knows he's never leaving this basement alive, no matter what. I guess the "good cop" routine is never going to work for me. I sigh and walk to the cinderblocks across from him where a gray panel is set into the wall.

"What's that?" An edge of worry creeps into his words.

"Power control."

"For what?"

I open the small gray breaker panel. "Sump pump." Glancing at him over my shoulder, I flip the switch. A low, almost inaudible hum dies off, leaving us both in total silence.

His gaze lowers to the concrete floor, the cracks already wet with the boggy water that's impossible to keep out even during a drought. The bayou is never far away, not even here on my thickly-treed property. In a few hours, the water will cover the entire floor by at least an inch.

I press my boot to the seat of his chair and kick. He falls backward with a clang, and his scream is just as high and sharp as usual. I suppose the barbed wire digging into him plus having his hands crushed beneath him is more than a little uncomfortable.

I shrug and stare down at him as his cries die off. "It's funny. When I had this house built, my architect told me there was no way I could have a basement in this part of Louisiana. Too much water in the ground. He said the water table is so close to the surface that this space would fill in no time, especially if there isn't a heavy-duty pump to keep it dry." I grin and tap my foot into the puddle beside me. "But here we are in my very own basement, so joke's on him, am I right?"

His ruined eyes widen, understanding finally hitting him in his gut. "Lucius, you can't leave me here like this. The water—"

"I'll be back in the morning." I head to the stairs, not even bothering to look at him. "I expect you to talk if you haven't drowned by then. And if you have—" I shrug. "Keep hell warm for me."

2

EVELYN

Lucius stalks around his home like some sort of aggressive beast, never staying in any one room too long. I watch him stride through the living room, his phone at his ear, anger telegraphing through each of his steps. Out here in this solitary stretch of land, he doesn't even bother hanging curtains or blinds. The steel and glass monstrosity of his ultra-modern home jut and shine, and he prowls through the entirety of it like a tiger in a zoo enclosure ... If the zoo invested in bullet-proof glass, anyway.

I lean against a moss-strewn oak and resist the urge to unzip my jacket and let the humid air circulate through. Darkness is my friend, and the lighter shirt beneath my black jacket wouldn't be a prudent look. Even though his house is lit, and he's not looking my way, I have the creeping sensation that he knows I'm out here. That's ridiculous, of course. I've covered my tracks again and again. No one knows where I am. Besides, there's no one left who would care.

He ends his call, then turns toward me, his gaze on the patch of woods where I watch and wait. He's too far away for me to see what he's looking at precisely, but it's a hard enough stare that I shrink behind the tree a little more. He watches for agonizing seconds, each moment lasting longer and longer as I foolishly hold my breath. He can't see me, can't hear me, I remind myself.

I slide my hand into my pocket, the cold gunmetal reassuring me that it doesn't matter what Lucius does, his end is coming soon. I've waited a long time for this, and if I need to wait a little longer to find an opening? So be it. I'll be ready. And I won't miss.

Skulking around his house in the dark is just part of my reconnaissance. There's plenty more for me to do before I can deal my death blow. The machinery is already in motion, and I want to twist all the screws, to make him bleed, to cut him into a thousand slices of agony. And when I'm done? I'll fade away into the night and start fresh somewhere else. Once he's dead, I'll be rid of the nightmares that wake me screaming. No more memories, no more regrets. Justice will be done, and I'll be the one to watch his eyes fog over, to witness the moment his particular form of malignancy dies.

An icy trickle of worry slides down my spine. I snap out of my bloodlust and return my gaze to the window.

Fuck.

He's gone.

3

LUCIUS

I weave through the trees at the edge of my lawn, my pistol up and ready. That feeling of being watched grew a little too heavy—or perhaps I needed a little energy release after that phone call with my brother Sin—so I decided to try and get the drop on my ghost.

If Sin had only listened to me when I said I didn't want to take our company public, we wouldn't be in this one of our many messes. But now we've got sharks circling us, trying to take down the sugar empire our mother built. I let out a deep breath and focus on the here and now. My tension falls away as I skirt the lawn in the dark. The ghost is here, a spectral form that teases the edge of my senses.

I should've let it go, drank myself into a stupor, gone to bed. Instead, I came ghost-hunting. Tension relief. Besides, it'll be fun to have another captive in my basement. Give soggy Leonard some company.

Keeping my steps as silent as possible, I circle around to the spot where I suspect the ghost is waiting. The moon gives just enough light for me to follow a slight trail toward an old oak. Bent grass and the edge of a shoeprint sit in a boggy spot next to the roots. Someone's been here, but they're gone now.

I lower my weapon but keep it handy as I scour the area for any clues. Nothing remains, except the scant evidence on the ground. It's too dark to follow the trail deeper into the trees, but I suspect he's parking a car on the dirt road that cuts through the property just to the south of mine, then walking here.

I take a deep breath to smooth away my frustration. Why can't I be patient like old Casper? If he saw me coming, he won't be back to this spot. I've spooked the ghost. Shit.

Resting against the oak tree with the trampled ground, I peer at my house. From here, he can see everything. Not that I care. If someone wants to come for me, they know where to find me. It's not hard. I relish a fight, and confrontation has always looked good on me. But I'm not stupid. The house has enough security to please any paranoia enthusiast. Even so, I still run to a fight. Here I am, in the woods like a rash fool. I turn to leave.

A twig breaking catches my attention, and without thinking, I dart deeper into the woods, running toward my ghost with my gun at the ready. Footsteps sound ahead. He's running. I grin, because I know these woods better than anyone, and I can find him even in the dark. I follow the footfalls, racing to catch up, but then they stop.

I stop, too. He's gone to ground—hiding behind a tree or hunkering under a thorny thicket. I'm breathing hard, but I'm not winded. I swallow the cool air and scan through the leafy saplings and climbing brambles.

"I know you're here." I rest my hand on a tree trunk. "And I'll get you soon enough."

"Not if I get you first." A woman's voice that's far too close behind me.

I whirl to find the ghost, her gun aimed at my heart. A black ski mask covers her face, but there's no doubt in my mind she's all woman based on the way her dark jacket and jeans hug her curves. Don't they say that people in life-or-death situations always stare at the gun? Right at the barrel? Not me, apparently. I stare at the woman holding it.

"Drop your gun." She squares her stance as if she's at a shooting range.

"You first." I smile but don't raise my weapon. I'm curious to see how this goes. A little danger can be the best aphrodisiac.

"I'm not kidding, asshole." Her accent is local. She's from here, or at least nearby.

"Okay." I take a step toward her.

She doesn't move. "I wouldn't do that if I were you."

"Why not?"

"Because if you come any closer, I'll drop you. I didn't want to kill you tonight. Not yet. But you had to go and get nosy."

"Sounds like you're going to have to shoot me no matter what."

Her eyes narrow, though I can't tell their color in the shadows of her mask. "You want me to kill you?"

"Don't flatter yourself. You have no idea how many have tried to take me out. Each one has failed. Though I admit, you're the first woman." I try to glimpse her hair, but she has it tied up beneath the mask. "I should've known anyone as patient as you had to be a woman. I only wish I'd seen you sooner." My gaze travels down her body once again. Damn, even in black, in the dark—she's stacked. "Just look at you."

"Are you ... flirting?" Her finger caresses the trigger.

"Just stating facts." I can feel the blood thrumming through my veins. This little taste of danger hits me in all the right places, and I wonder what my would-be assassin looks like under the mask. "Let's drop this whole murderer routine and head back to my house, darlin'." I give her my most disarming smile. "We can talk about whatever beef you have over some cocktails, and then I'll show you why killing me would be a great disservice to the women of the world."

"I knew it wouldn't be hard to pull the trigger, but you're making it so much easier for me."

"So you're a hardened killer?" I take another step toward her. "I'm not your first?"

"Stop."

"Because I think you've never killed anyone." I take another step.

"Stop!"

"If you had, I'd already be dead. You would've shot me in the back before I even turned around." I chance another step.

She pushes the gun out toward me even farther. "I'll do it!" Despite her bravado, I can hear the tremor in her voice. She isn't ready to take a life, not even mine. What the fuck is she doing out here? And who is she?

I have to decide whether to rush her or shoot her, so I run my mouth some more to buy time. "I've killed plenty. With a gun, my hands, a cane knife." I shake my head. "That last one is pretty brutal. You ever seen a cane knife? It's what you use to harvest sugar cane, sort of like a machete crossed with a meat cleaver. Sharp, heavy. A skull cracks like a coconut if you hit it just right."

"I already know you're a monster." Her tone burns like acid. "You don't have to do any more convincing."

"Not a monster. Just efficient. And if I'm threatened —" I advance again, close enough to tackle her. "I react. And I keep reacting until the threat is room temperature."

She lets out a deep breath, as if she's trained for this moment. "I told you to stop."

"How about you put the gun down, we get out our aggressions on each other, and then—"

Her glare intensifies. "You're *still* trying to make a pass?"

"Not a pass. I'm offering to fuck you, to give you what you need so hard that you beg me to stop. Something tells me you need a good, rough fuck to knock some sense into you. Because you aren't a killer. You're something else. Something I want." The black hides her, but not enough. I can see the swells of her full breasts, the flare of her hips, the way her pants hug the sweet spot between her thighs. Damn. "How about this—let me get you off, then you can shoot me. Sound good?" I edge closer.

"I said stop!"

I give her a smirk, the one I already know tends to infuriate its recipient. "Darlin', I never stop." I lunge for her.

The gun blast knocks me off my feet.

4
EVELYN

I shot him.

I yank my mask off and toss it into the passenger seat as I start the car.

I. Shot. Him.

A laugh bubbles out of me, tickling along my lips and growing until I'm giggling. He's dead. I killed Lucius Vinemont. The bitterest sugar magnate is no more, and I was the one who finally dealt him the justice he deserved. The giggles overtake me, and I'm laughing so hard that my ribs hurt, and I can barely breathe.

"Oh my god!" I bang on the steering wheel, joy and adrenaline mixing inside me until I'm whooping at the top of my lungs. I shot him in the heart, just like I'd practiced so many times at the shooting range. He fell back, his body going limp. Dead.

Another squeal rips from me, and I slump in my

seat, relief welling as I consider what this means to me. All these years spent with one goal in mind, one endgame. And it happened. It was *easy*. So easy to take his life. Nothing like all the scenarios I'd played out and trained for. No, I snuffed him out like someone cutting the head off a snake.

Justice. That's what it was. Right? Yes. It *has* to be. My laughter turns into tears so quickly I wonder if I'm cracking under the pressure. I wail into my hands. Tears of joy, relief, and maybe finally, closure?

I don't know, but the emotions that I've had bottled up for so long are free now, and I let the tears flow until I can't breathe without sobbing. After what feels like an hour but is more like a few minutes, I reel it in, letting the explosion of feelings dissipate as I catch my breath and blow my nose. I can only hope the weight of grief is finally lifting, the promise of a new beginning shining brightly. I did what I came to do. Revenge served cold. I can leave Lucius behind. Finally.

I spend a few more minutes quietly blubbering before blowing my nose again and composing myself as best I can. There's so much to do. First, I need to ditch the gun, burn my clothes, and make sure my ass is covered. Someone will discover the body soon enough. I need to be back in New Orleans before that happens. Besides, I have an appointment in the morning with the board of Magnolia Sugar to lay out the benefits of them siding with me on the hostile takeover. I may have killed Lucius sooner than I planned, but I still intend to bring the entire Vinemont empire crashing to the ground. I won't kill the other two brothers. Lucius was the only one who had to die. But if they cross me, I might change my mind. After all, I'm a killer now. What's a few more notches on my gun?

God, I'd had this whole speech prepared for him. It wasn't "*my name is Inigo Montoya*" great or anything, but it laid out his sins against me. I didn't have the chance to utter a word of it. It was just over, done, the end. One minute he was breathing, the next I'd taken his twisted life. So easy.

I shouldn't dwell on it, not when I have more plans. I'll have a bottle of prosecco and a long bath when I'm safe in my loft, not sitting out here in the parish I used to roam.

Pulling down my mirror, I swipe the wetness from below my eyes and blink hard a few times. "You can do this. You proved it," I tell myself. "You're not some weak girl who just lets things happen to her. You're strong. You make your destiny."

With a deep breath, I stow the gun in the glove box and start the car.

My new world is just beginning, and it's so much brighter now that Lucius Vinemont isn't in it.

5

LUCIUS

She shot me. *She fucking shot me!*
I sit up and feel my ruined shirt and the vest beneath. This is worse than being kicked by a horse.

"Jesus." I cough and half expect to spit blood. The bullet didn't knock me out, but I sure as hell played dead so she wouldn't add a slug to my face. But I didn't need to worry. She stood there for a few seconds, seemingly shocked into silence, and then took off through the woods.

Like I said, she isn't a stone-cold killer. If she were, she would have made sure I never drew another breath. Instead, she ran off, scared and full of adrenaline, not thinking straight.

I struggle to my feet, the pain in my chest radiating to my ribs and around my back. "Fucking hell." I lean against the tree.

What did I do to this woman? I yank my shirt open and reach for the straps holding my vest in place. She wasn't familiar, not that I could see much. But she's got some major anger issues where I'm concerned. She wanted to kill me herself, not hire it out to a contract killer or watch from afar. No, this was personal for her. But who the fuck is she?

I've wronged plenty of women in my life, mainly by making promises I never intend to keep. Once I get them in bed, I'm done. I'm the typical asshole who lives for the chase, and once I've gotten a taste of my kill, I move on to the next. But I can't imagine that any of those women could be *this* pissed at me. After all, I make them come—usually many times over—before I take my leave.

I finally free myself from the vest and throw it down. A red bruise takes shape over my heart. It'll be black and blue in a few hours.

Walking gingerly, I return to my house and pour another bourbon. I'm going to have to finish this bottle to make a dent in the pain. Picking up my phone, I dial Sin.

"What the fuck do you want now?" My brother's classic coldness doesn't bother me.

"Someone tried to kill me tonight."

"Who?" He sounds almost bored.

"A woman."

"A toothy blowjob isn't a murder attempt, Lucius."

"Fuck you." I collapse into my favorite chair even though the movement amplifies my aches.

"One of your former conquests, I presume?"

"I don't think so." I pop back a couple of high-flying painkillers and down them with more bourbon. "This one had some major vengeance vibes going. She tapped me right in the heart. Vest was the only thing that saved me. But I can't place her."

"She didn't monologue first?" He sighs. "I usually monologue a little before I kill someone. Give them a little background, mainly to the tune of 'don't ever fuck with a Vinemont.' Seems she wasted a great opportunity."

"Didn't have a chance. It happened so fast. I spooked her into shooting me, more or less."

"God, you're a dumbass." He clears the sleep from his voice a bit more. "Think it has to do with Leonard and his band of merry miscreants?"

"Doubt it. She's been watching me for a while, long before I got my hands on that idiot downstairs."

"Is he suffering enough? Or do I need to come take care of it?"

"Take care of your family. I'll handle the heavy lifting."

I can feel him bristling through the phone. "You think I can't handle th—"

"*What is it?*" Stella, my brother's wife, mumbles sleepily in the background.

"Nothing, go on back to sleep."

"*Is Lucius okay?*"

"He's fine. Just got a woman trying to kill him."

She laughs. "*Why am I not surprised?*"

"Actually, don't go back to sleep just yet." A loud smack and a squeal sound through the line.

I roll my eyes. How can two people still be so in love after five years, not to mention all the shit Sin and Stella have been through?

"Is that all you had to tell me?" Sin asks. "We have to be at the attorneys' tomorrow first thing, and I have some business to take care of at the moment."

"The failed murder attempt was the reason for my call, yes."

"You're alive. Quit bitching... Stella, my love, get on all fours. Now." The line goes silent.

"Motherfucker." I toss my phone down and light up a joint.

I go back through the encounter with my would-be assassin, doing my best to place her. I got nothing. Nothing except what feels like a few cracked ribs, but of course the booze, narcotics, and hopefully the weed will ease the pain.

"I'm alive, darlin'. Though you certainly tried it." I lift my glass to her. She should've known you can't use a bullet to kill the devil. It'll take a whole hell of a lot more to put me down.

"What did I do to you?" I smile. It's the only action that doesn't hurt. "Whatever it was, I made an impression." Inhaling, I hold the smoke in and picture her eyes in the black mask, the slight waver of her voice, the way she tried to be aggressive when everything inside me was yelling that what she needed was a ferocious animal fuck right there in the woods.

My cock is hard. Because I'm twisted. Because just the thought of overpowering her is like a shot of adrenaline through my system. I've never wanted a woman so badly in my life, and I don't even know who she is. But a man like me doesn't let go. Not when he gets on a scent as interesting as this one. She's my quarry, and I intend to track her down and have another chat, preferably one where she's bent over and moaning while I ram my cock deep inside her. Maybe it'll end with one of us dead, but I suspect it'll be worth it.

I blow out the puff of smoke. "The good news is, you're still out there, darlin'. The bad news is, I'm coming for you."

6

EVELYN

"I thought you wanted to remain silent in this?" My lawyer, Linton Graves, brushes nonexistent lint from his impeccable dark gray suit.

"I've changed my mind." I smooth my blonde hair back and straighten my skirt. "The impediment I mentioned before is gone, so I can have an active role from this point forward."

"Are you certain that's what you want?" He peers down his too-sharp nose at me. "The Vinemonts are not too happy with your hostile takeover, and they aren't particularly kind to their enemies."

"I can handle them." *The two that are left.*

"Plenty have said that, and plenty have been incorrect. Sinclair, the eldest, is an arrogant, condescending brute. But Lucius, the next in line, is particularly nasty."

"And the third?" I already know the particulars of

each brother, but it's interesting to watch Linton try to school me.

"Teddy?" He waves a manicured hand. "He has no real involvement in the family business since he's in his residency, but he will back his brothers fiercely and defend his one-third interest in Magnolia Sugar. Don't fall for his charm, Ms. Delacroix. He's still a Vinemont and will cut the legs out from under you if given half a chance."

"Then let's not give them the chance." I throw my shoulders back and hope he doesn't notice the dark circles under my eyes. Sleep never came last night, and I couldn't stop thinking about the surprised yet bemused look on Lucius's face when I took his life.

I thought I'd slumber more deeply than I ever had, but instead I tossed and turned. Something niggled at me, a worrisome sense of guilt that was utterly out of place. I shouldn't feel sorry for Lucius, not after what he's done. For all I know, it was him or me at that point. He had a gun, and he came after me. I did what I had to do. No, I chided myself; I did what I *planned* to do all along. Everything had gone according to my plan, even if it was a little early. I am in control.

"Everything all right?" Linton is peering at me a little too closely.

"Fine." I grab the door handle and turn it, entering the main area of the high-priced law firm. My heels clack along the polished marble floor as I stride to the largest conference room—the neutral space where I intend to convince the board of Magnolia Sugar to accept my purchase offer. Morning sun shines into the skyscraper via the floor-to-ceiling windows, and every bit of décor screams wealth. This is where the rich come to do business.

"Allow me." Linton cuts in front of me and pulls open the glass door to the conference room.

I stride in and analyze the space, the long marble table, the leather chairs, the neat set of portfolios laid out for each board member. This is the show, and I'm the one calling the shots. It's almost laughable, especially considering I was groomed to be a rich man's bride, a silent accessory, a trophy to be dusted off only when it was time to make the children and further his line. Instead of that nightmare, fate—or more accurately, the Vinemonts—dealt me an entirely different path, one fraught with thorns and pain, but which eventually led to the light. To freedom. And now here I stand, about to take my enemy's empire from them and crush it in my grasp.

"If you're ready, I'll get the board." Linton straightens the documents in front of my seat, squaring them perfectly with the edge of the table. His precision is one of the reasons I hired him. "They're having coffee and scones in the breakfast room. Probably done by now."

I run my hands along the marble tabletop. "I'm ready."

He steps out, and I steel my nerves, forcing myself

to remember that I'm in charge of my fate now. No one else. The main obstacle is already gone, and now all I have left to do is finish the rest of the Vinemont clan. Financial ruin will be a good start.

The door opens, and I turn to meet each board member as they file in. Handshakes and smiles are exchanged as the six men enter and take their seats. A transcriptionist sits in one corner and sets up her machine. Three chairs are left open—one for Lucius, chairman of the board. I try not to smirk at the knowledge that he won't make it today. The other two are for Sinclair and Teddy, both invited to the board meeting as a matter of cordiality.

"We may as well get started." I glance at Linton and jerk my chin toward the door.

He closes it and joins me at the table.

"We need to wait for Lucius." One of the board members wipes crumbs from his coat.

"I think we all know how he feels about the offer from Delacroix. Him being here won't change anything."

He stops wiping. "And you are?"

"My apologies." Linton steps to his seat. "This is Evelyn Delacroix, the head of Delacroix Enterprises."

The board member rubs his salt and pepper beard. "I thought that other guy, the one with the glasses—"

"Mr. Frankfurt is the CEO, but Evelyn is the owner. We planned on having this meeting a bit later in the process when the intricacies of our corporate structure became more important, but Ms. Delacroix wanted to go ahead and get acquainted with all of you." Linton offers a comfortable smile, one that—along with his reasonable tone—has defused plenty of disputes.

The board member, Mr. Van from my research, doesn't buy it. "We still should wait for Lucius. If we started without him, he wouldn't appreciate it."

I wave my hand toward the empty leather chairs. "It's clearly not as important to the Vinemonts as it is to all of you. After all, your time is valuable, isn't it? Yet you're here in a timely fashion." I break out my own smile, the girlish one I hate because it reminds me of the old me. "And I'm genuinely excited about this opportunity and the benefits it can afford to everyone at this table. I'd be happy to speak with Lucius separately and go over the specifics, though I'm sure he'll be here any moment."

Mr. Van casts a look at my cleavage even though I'm dressed rather demurely, the neck of my white blouse in a modest scoop and my dark skirt suit form-fitting but classy. My hands go cold as he considers me, and I remember how much I hate being seen.

Finally, he says, "I suppose we could start. Like you said, he'll be here soon."

"Thank you." I look around the room, meeting each board member's eyes. "If you'll turn to page one of the prospectus, you'll see the particulars of the deal Delacroix is offering. I think you'll find that my offer will lead to a nice payout for the shareholders. My company has a short but strong history of taking companies from low or medium performing positions and, for lack of a better phrase, turbo-charging them. We trim the fat, get rid of any sentimentality or entrenched management, and do what's required to turn bigger profits year after year. On page two, you'll see the results we achieved from acquiring Parade Pecans two years ago. That was a complete turnaround, from barely performing to becoming the number one pecan supplier for all grocery stores in the southeast. The Kincaid family had owned that business since the Great Depression, but the sons and grandsons had run it into the ground. Tradition kept the board from replacing them. But I changed all that, and now its balance sheets are the envy of its competitors. Now, what I'm offering—"

The glass door to my right swings open and I turn. Sinclair and Teddy Vinemont stroll in. Sinclair doesn't even look at me, and Teddy gives me a neutral expression as they walk to the empty seats.

"Began without us?" Sinclair sinks down and steeples his fingers before giving me an appraising glance. "And having your college intern give your sales pitch?" He smirks.

"This is Evelyn Delacroix," Linton says, his calm tone almost grating. "She's the owner of Del—"

"Delacroix. Yes, I follow." Sinclair flicks the prospectus across the table where it lands at the transcriptionist's feet. "I trust the board knows what's best for this company. The same thing that's been best for this company for decades—the Vinemonts."

I clear my throat and look everywhere but at the brothers. "As I was saying, Parade Pecans was drowning in debt, had distribution problems, and an entrenched family at the top levels. However, once Delacroix took charge—"

"Not going to wait for the chairman of the board?" Sinclair's smirk is still in place.

He's not coming. "This meeting started at eight. If the chairman was interested in the future of his company, then he'd be here. As it is ..." I smile, but this time all my girlishness is gone. "As I said, when families become entrenched at the top of an organization, the business tends to suffer as do its investors. Delacroix is here to help."

Sinclair chuckles low in his throat, then pins me with his gaze again. His eyes narrow. "Don't I know you, Ms. Delacroix?"

The hair on the back of my neck rises, but not because of his question. No. It's because of the heavy footsteps I hear in the hall and the shadow that falls across the glass door.

I turn and freeze as Lucius Vinemont pulls the door open with a slight wince.

Alive. He's alive.

He strides to the open chair and takes his seat, then levels a Cheshire grin at me. "So, Evelyn, what did I miss?"

7
LUCIUS

It's her. My mind whispers that phrase over and over as Evelyn Delacroix gives her pitch to the board about why we should allow her to take control of the company. I can't concentrate on her numbers, because I'm far too busy with her figure. It's the one from last night. Same high, round tits and hips that are made for a man like me. The same one that tried to put a bullet in my heart.

I scrutinize her face. She's familiar, but I'd remember a woman like her if I'd ever had her underneath me. Who is she?

I pull out my phone and look at the dossier prepared by our attorneys concerning her company. Plenty of capital on-hand, good financials, strong performance. I flip to the page on management but find only a generic paragraph about Evelyn. No information, no notion of where the hell she came from except for receiving a degree from some Northeastern blueblood school and moving right into starting her own company and making a mint. How the fuck does a twenty-four-year-old manage that on her own?

"Magnolia's cash on hand and rare property holdings make it a perfect target for plenty of other companies to buy it up. After all, you own or lease some of the most productive sugar cane plantations in the world. But—" She shoots a pointed look at me. "You're also bogged down by a heavy-handed family that is entrenched in the business to its detriment. As primary shareholder, Delacroix would revamp Magnolia until it is performing at its most profitable levels. However, should you refuse this offer, who's to say that another firm won't come along, win a proxy fight, take the company, then sell off the lands, leases, and assets piece by piece until there's nothing left?"

She flips to a page in her prospectus. "The answer is 'you can't'. But that's where I can ..."

I shoot Sin a text.

Lucius: She's the one.

He arches a brow then responds.

Sinclair: You going to propose?

Lucius: No, asshole. She's the one who tried to kill me last night.

Sinclair: She's trying to kill this company right now.

" ... numbers clearly show there is plenty of room for improvement to—"

"Ms. Delacroix, sorry to interrupt, but you have absolutely zero knowledge of what it takes to run a business like this." I keep my tone level.

She turns to me, her blue eyes keen in the morning light. "My degrees and track record say otherwise. Whereas you have nothing other than wealth and a company handed down to you, I have the ability to understand the inner workings and make changes for the better. Your family ties to this business are a noose around its neck."

I stand, looming over her. "A bullet through its heart, you mean?"

She swallows hard but doesn't back down. "Use whatever turn of phrase you like, Mr. Vinemont, but this company is not living up to its shareholders' expectations. If it were, I wouldn't be here."

Jesus Christ. Who is this woman? She looks soft and inviting, but her teeth are sharp and her claws? They leave fucking marks. I wouldn't mind having a few on me.

"Let's call this what it is, Ms. Delacroix—a hostile takeover wrapped in a pretty package." I let my gaze slide down her body, then back to her eyes. "You're here because your company preys on shareholder doubts and multiplies them until you've created a problem to which you're the only solution. I see your sleight of hand, and I can assure you the board will as well."

Though her cheeks turn a brighter shade of pink,

she stands her ground. "The board serves at the pleasure of the shareholders, and I will have the proxy votes to change leadership by the time the shareholder meeting happens in May if you refuse to accept my offer as it stands." She turns to the rest of the board, and I can see her heartbeat fluttering at her throat.

Despite her calm demeanor, she feels the fight in her veins. She's a predator like me, and when she scents blood, she doesn't stop. I like it—her fire, her violence. I want more if it, and isn't that a fucking problem.

"I would advise you all to consider my proposal and let Delacroix help you instead of remaining captive to old money interests who serve only themselves." She shoots me a sharp glance. "Thank you for your time." She collects her bag and her attorney, then the two of them leave the conference room.

I turn to the board and stroll to the head of the table. "Look, she did a great song and dance. Really, she did. I appreciated it as much as all of you. But the simple fact is, her company is far too wet behind the ears to take on Magnolia. She may have ideas or thoughts on improving our business, but I didn't hear a single concrete idea that would increase profits." I point at Sin. "That's because we know this business inside and out. Call us old money if you want, but our family built this company brick by brick, doing whatever was necessary to see it succeed and thrive. If you think allying with Delacroix is in your best interest ..."

I take in a deep breath and stare down each board member in turn. "I suggest you rethink your position and consider your future as a well-paid member of our board." I retake my chair. "Meeting's over. Give us the room."

I'm not interested in their thoughts on the matter. After all, I just gave them all the thoughts they need on the matter. If someone isn't on the same page, I'll have to pay a visit to them outside of business hours. It's always work, work, work, isn't it?

I lean back as they file out and the transcriptionist follows, leaving Sin, Teddy, and me in the room.

"You let that little slip of a woman get the drop on you?" Sin smirks.

"Shut up."

Teddy shrugs. "She didn't convince the board. I don't see a problem."

I lean back and peer out at the foyer. Evelyn's in deep conversation with her attorney.

"She may not have convinced the board, but if she can get proxies from shareholders, she can install her own board." I idly flip through her prospectus. "But that's not even the point. The point is that she tried to kill me last night, and I have no clue why."

"What?" Teddy's blond eyebrows rise in alarm.

I wave a hand at him. "It was nothing."

"Nothing?" He stands. "Are you shot? Do I need to check you—"

"I'm fine, doc. Just a little bruised. Sit your *Grey's Anatomy* ass down."

He gives me a sharp look. "Dick."

"She was wearing a mask, so I didn't see her face, but it's her. I can feel it." Like an animal scenting its prey—I *know* it was her.

I glance at her again. She's moving, heading toward the elevator bank, and her sidekick is already gone. There's no way I'm letting her get away this easily.

"You two discuss reasons amongst yourselves. I'm going to have a little chat with Ms. Delacroix."

"Lucius," Sin says in his bored drawl.

"What?" I pull the door open.

"Try not to leave any forensic evidence this time." He stands and buttons his suit coat.

Teddy shakes his head. "Don't you do anything, Lucius. You can't even be sure it was her."

"Me? Why, I wouldn't hurt anyone, Teddy. You know that. Sugar wouldn't melt in my mouth." I let the door close as Sin barks a laugh and Teddy fumbles for a comeback.

Evelyn thinks she has the upper hand. That's cute. It really is. But if she knows me at all—and she must—she should know I'm more than happy to turn the screw until she shows me every secret in her cunning mind.

8

EVELYN

The elevator only drops one floor before stopping and opening again. I scoot back a few steps as a young man in an impeccable suit steps on, his bright blue eyes catching mine as he casually leans against the wall beside me. He's too close. The entire car is open, but he's invading my personal space. Unfortunately for him, I made a decision that I will not be intimidated ever again. So, I stand my ground.

"I wonder."

His voice surprises me, but I don't make any movement or let it show.

He continues, "I wonder if you ever miss your brother?"

My throat closes, and I hold his gaze. I didn't pack a weapon for the board meeting. Maybe I should have.

"Excuse me?" I glance at the elevator numbers as we get closer to the lobby and freedom.

"Red Witherington. Your brother. Do you feel bad he's gone?" He moves quickly, caging me in against the back wall.

My heart slams against my ribs as I clutch my useless bag. I know how to fight. I've taken self-defense classes for just this moment. But one thing learning and sparring doesn't prepare you for is the fear. Looking up at the man who's easily twice my size, the fear is what keeps me in place, my heart rampaging in my chest.

"I asked you a question, Evie." He uses the nickname that Red gave me, the one I left behind in the fire that burned down my entire world.

"Who are you?" My voice trembles, and I hate that he can hear it.

"Your future." He smiles, slow and easy, his perfectly straight teeth a testament to modern orthodontia.

The elevator slows as we approach the bottom floor, and he backs off and adjusts his tie. "It was a pleasure meeting you, Evie. We'll be in touch." He pulls a black envelope from his inner suit pocket and holds it out.

The doors begin to open as he thrusts it into my shaking hand.

"See you around." He turns and strolls toward the center of the building where a smattering of high-end stores and restaurants hum with businesspeople on early lunch breaks.

I stand there, fear rolling down my spine like ice water, until the doors close and the elevator begins moving upward. Taking in a shuddering breath, I jam my finger on the lobby button again, then carefully place the black envelope into my bag.

My mind is a cacophony of thoughts that boils down to one: *They found me.*

I'm not the woman I was, and I covered my tracks so, so well. But I should've known better. I was wondering if they'd been paying attention, and I was a fool to hope they weren't.

The elevator stops, and a woman gets on and gives me a warm smile. I can't return it, so hers fades like the bloom on a wilting flower as she stands near the door.

My stomach churns, and I fear I might be sick. When we're back to the lobby, I peek out but don't see the man with the golden hair and blue eyes.

Hurrying from the elevator, I take a hard right and speed my steps toward the parking deck. I need to get out of here, to save myself from my impending panic attack. It's building, each step bringing me closer to my car and also a breakdown.

My heart beats a vicious rhythm to the tune of: *They found me. They found me. They found me.* The whispers are true. It's happening again. Was that man the Sovereign? The envelope in my bag is like a ticking bomb, a burning fuse, a set of skeletal fingers around my ankle. I burst into the deck, my heels clacking on the concrete as I hurry to my Mercedes.

I pull up short when I see someone leaning against it. The man I killed is standing there and giving me a cocky smirk as I do my best to keep my breakfast from splashing on the ground.

"You don't look so good, Ms. Delacroix. Having trouble?" He rests against my driver's side door, blocking my escape.

"Move." Panic rides me hard, but I refuse to let him see it. I kick up my chin and march to him as I crumble to dust on the inside. "There are cameras all over this deck. You can't—"

He grips the front of my blouse and yanks me to him. I squeal and drop my bag.

"I *can*." His eyes blaze into me as he holds me close, close enough to kiss ... or kill. "I can do whatever the fuck I want to do, Ms. Delacroix. And let's be clear: I *know* it was you."

"I don't know what—"

"Don't lie to me, Evelyn." His nostrils flare. "*Never* lie to me. The devil always knows." His smirk returns as I try to push him away.

His other arm goes around my waist and he holds me tightly against him.

"Your heart is beating faster than a rabbit's. Afraid?" He grips my jaw, his gaze darting to my lips.

"I'm not afraid of you." I feel the tension in my body, but it's different now. Not the sick, sinking feeling from what happened on the elevator. Lucius makes me feel more. He always has, ever since I saw him when I was still a girl, when Red was still alive. Handsome and oh-so-bad, the cocky Lucius Vinemont was my teenage fantasy. Because I didn't know what bad was back then. Not really.

I do now. I know evil. I've seen it. And right now, the most evil man I've ever known has me crushed to his chest, his gaze darting to my lips. No, this fear is not the same as in the elevator, but I *wish* it was. I wish I had only fear and revulsion for him.

I wish I'd never set eyes on Lucius Vinemont.

"Not afraid of me?" He tsks. "If that's true, then you aren't as intelligent as you seem." He strokes my cheek with his thumb. "Because I will find you out, Evelyn Delacroix. I will learn your secrets and use them to destroy you. Soon enough, you'll be begging me for mercy, but I won't give you any."

"If you're done threatening me, I'd like to leave now."

"You sure?" He slides his hand to my throat and rests it there like a collar. "My offer from last night still stands. That prim little suit you're wearing would look even better on my bedroom floor."

"I don't know what you're talking about." I try to breathe, to clear the panic from my mind, to pretend the desire isn't there. I thought I'd killed it. Just like Lucius killed my entire family. That's what snaps me out of it. That memory of ash and crimson blood. I hate the man. Nothing more.

"Get off me." I grit the words between my teeth.

He squeezes my throat, but not too hard. "See you around, Evelyn." Releasing me, he backs up but stops only a few feet away.

His eyes burn into me as I fumble at the door handle, finally get it, then slide into the driver's seat and slam the door. I back out quickly and speed away, his gaze still on me until I turn at the end of the row and finally escape.

The panic attack hits me a few blocks later, and I have to park, open the door, and empty my guts onto the street. Cold sweat covers me as I sit back up and wipe my mouth on my sleeve. I reach into my bag for a tissue, but my fingers meet the envelope. I pull my hand back as if burned and fight another wave of nausea.

I can't do this, can't have anything to do with *them* again. As much as I hate the Vinemonts—and I do—I hate the Acquisition just as much. Cruel and wrong, it was the catalyst to my downfall, to everything that ended with the flare of a match in a Vinemont's fingers. I can almost smell the ash, the sickly scent of burning bodies. The look in my brother's dead eyes.

Opening my door again, I empty what little is left in my stomach, then slam the door and rest my head on the steering wheel. Skin clammy, body still trembling, I take deep breaths.

I can't run from this. Just like I can't run from Lucius now that he's found me. Now that I screwed up and overplayed my hand.

Foolish. I was so fucking *foolish* to think I could kill my nightmare with a simple bullet. Tears burn in my eyes, but I blink them away. I have to be strong. This changes nothing. I'm going to crush him, to leave his entire legacy in ruin. I have to. For Red and for me.

I take a deep breath and fight back the memories of Red's blood on Lucius's knife, of the way Lucius had killed him with an almost perfunctory motion. Lucius Vinemont dotted the i's, crossed his t's, and sank his blade into my brother's beating heart.

A sob tries to work its way from my throat, but I swallow it down. Down, down, down, so deep it will never see the light of day. I'm not Evie Witherington anymore. I'm Evelyn Delacroix. Not powerless, not weak.

"You have to face it. All of it." My words are as shaky as my resolve.

With a trembling hand, I pull the envelope from my bag. The edges are crisp, the paper expensive, the gold leaf likely real. My name—my real name, is written in a beautiful, sweeping hand. My stomach turns again. Shuddering, I stuff the letter back in my bag. I'll open it later, after I've had a drink or three. That's when I can face it. But not here. Not now. Not when I'm blindsided.

I expected Lucius. I expected his evil. But this? This beautiful piece of paper is worse than all the Vinemonts combined.

9
LUCIUS

*I*t doesn't take long for my informants to begin searching for Evelyn Delacroix. I pay well for all my underworld contacts, and they've never failed me when it comes to sniffing out my enemies. Soon enough, I'll know why she's so fucking pissed at me.

I down a whiskey as I search through the information I've already amassed.

"If you keep drinking like that, your liver—"

"Yeah, yeah, go play Operation, okay?" I wave Teddy away.

"What?" He wrinkles his nose.

Teddy's living out of my New Orleans penthouse while he does his residency. I stay here whenever I'm in town. High atop the Ritz, this place is decked out with every comfort imaginable. Twenty-four hour room service I don't order, a view I don't bother to look at, and plenty of women and coke at my fingertips. Even so, I still prefer my estate back in the parish. New Orleans is just a necessary evil at this point, a place where I do business.

"*Operation*, Teddy boy. It's a great game for doctor types like you. Just don't touch the sides. When his nose lights up, you're fucked. Okay, buddy?"

"Such an asshole," Teddy mutters as he grabs a vitamin water from the fridge.

"That's no way to address your favorite big brother." I give him a grin.

"Sin's my favorite. Everyone knows that."

"Lies." I shrug, but the motion reignites the ache from Evelyn's bullet. She really got me. That fucking vixen with brass balls nailed me good.

"I can check that for you." He jerks his chin at me.

"I have all the medicine I need." I pour another whiskey.

He sighs. "You're going to die."

"So are you."

"You know what I mean." He downs some more of his healthy water bullshit.

I open an email from another informant. Looks like Evelyn Delacroix *did* attend Princeton, but funnily enough, the student ID photo shows a girl who is most definitely not the person I met today.

"That's not her." Teddy leans over behind me and looks at my screen. I'd bite Sin's head off for doing that shit, but Teddy gets a pass. He's the baby of the family, and now it appears I have to regain my 'favorite big brother' status. *Fuck*.

"Brilliant observation skills."

He doesn't respond to my crack. "She didn't get a degree. She's just ... Who is she?" he asks. "Do you think she was a part of *it*?" he asks quietly.

It. I know exactly what 'it' is. The Acquisition. A fucking contest between the snakes of southern society to decide who gets to lord over our tainted world. Modern slavery with mindfuckery twists and kinks worthy of a serial killer documentary. My brother Sin was the last Vinemont to participate in it, and we thought we'd killed the entire thing. But really, we'd only cut the head off the snake. I drink some more. No one should have to deal with this shit sober.

I finally get back to his question, to one of the myriad problems swirling around my beautiful little Ms. Delacroix. "I don't know. She could be." I sure as hell wish I did. "She's still young, though. Too young to have been involved directly, and if she had been, she'd be a pile of ash right now with all the rest of them."

He shakes his head. "She seemed familiar, though. Like I'd seen her before. But, then again, I see a lot of people at the hospital."

"See? That shit right there is just so goddamn intriguing." I rub the stubble that's already growing along my jaw. "Sin said she was familiar, too. Even *I'm* beginning to think maybe she's familiar. But how could

I have come near a woman like that and not fucked her? It doesn't make sense."

"That's ... that's the question you're left with?" He slides his palms down his cheeks.

I shrug.

"The more *important* question is, if all three of us suspect we've seen her before, is that a good sign? I don't think so." He pulls at my collar.

"No free peeks." I smack his hand away.

"Just let me look at the bruise, you big baby."

"This is stupid." I groan and place my laptop on the couch beside me and strip out of my dress shirt.

"Holy shit." He crosses his arms as he comes around to get a better look. The bruise is almost black with a yellow halo around the edges. Ugly, and about the size of a saucer, it's going to take a while for it to fade.

"Like it?" I ask.

"She could've stopped your heart. You know that? Could've thrown off the rhythm with the impact, and you'd be dead without the bullet ever breaking your skin."

I grimace. "That would've been anticlimactic."

"It's not a joke, Lucius."

I meet his gaze. He's still young. Has a good heart. Nothing like Sin and me. I want him to stay that way. "Look, you know how many people I've ... *dealt with* in the past. This is nothing new."

"I know." He gives me a stern nod. "Of course I

know. But this is different. You let her get close. Close enough to almost end your life. That's never happened before. You underestimated her, and it almost got you killed."

"It wasn't underestimation. It was more of a—I don't know—"

"I saw the way you were looking at her." He sighs.

I smirk. No point denying it. I want a taste, even if it's poisonous as fuck.

"You're a lost cause." His tone is almost sad, and I definitely detect disappointment in his puppy dog eyes. "I'll get some ice for the bruise. You may even have a sternum fracture. Hard to say without imaging." He strides to the kitchen.

I'm just glad he didn't spit out some bullshit about me going in for a—

"You know, it wouldn't hurt for you to get seen by …"

I ignore the rest of what he says and pull my laptop back to me. Another email has popped up. I delight in receiving information, and even more so now that I have such an interesting target. One with a body I wanted to bend over that boardroom table, not giving a shit about the consequences. Evelyn's good looking, no two ways about it, but more than that, she's got some fucking steel in her spine. Some fight. And fuck, my cock twitches to life just thinking about the way she felt in my arms. Pulse racing, her lips parted, fear and anger in her eyes, like she wanted to run but also stab me through the heart at the same time.

Teddy wraps the ice pack around my chest as I keep reading. Before I know it, it's afternoon, and I'm not much closer to finding out Evelyn's true identity. I've learned quite a bit, though. Where she lives, her habits, her recent past, and a few interesting tidbits about what she's done with the companies she's strong-armed.

Her schtick wasn't just a schtick. She might not be the real Evelyn Delacroix with an MBA, but she knows what she's doing. She doesn't break up companies and sell them off like a lot of bloodthirsty capitalists do. Her numbers add up, and she's pulled two companies from the brink of extinction.

"Teddy, I need another bottle." I hold up the empty whiskey, then look around. "Teddy?" Shit, he must be back at the hospital. The little prick is saving lives when he should be here refilling my glass.

My phone pings, and I check the message. More information, none of it particularly vital.

Private number: Evelyn Delacroix is a ghost. I've tracked her back to her first position working for a hedge fund in New York. She climbs the ranks, bounces around from bank to bank, then goes out on her own. She pulled the capital from an account in the Caymans to start her business, but that's as far as I could go.

An account in the fucking Caymans? Is she a drug

kingpin? If so, I'm down. But something tells me that's not the case. There'd be no reason for her to come after me. I trade in sugar, not the other white stuff. Not to say I haven't done a ton of dirt in my life. I have. My hands are covered in blood, so it's not unusual that someone would show up with a grudge against me. It's happened before. Just not like this.

No, Evelyn's a much more complicated puzzle than simple money, business acumen, and an unexplained thirst for vengeance. At least I'm the only one she's after. She didn't look twice at Sin or Teddy, but I felt her staring daggers at me. I really wish I knew why she had such a hard-on for my blood.

Not that it bothers me. Not at all. I smile. I like her violence. She wants my blood. I like that, too. When I get her on all fours, I want her to hate how much she loves me fucking her.

I toss the laptop beside me and lean back, the ache in my chest still there but also sort of numb thanks to the ice. Every pulse of pain reminds me of that minx.

"Who are you, Evelyn?" I ask the empty penthouse. "And what the fuck did I do to you?"

10

EVELYN

After a sleepless night, I'm staring at the alarm clock when it starts to beep. I hit the off button, then snuggle back into my pillow, one hand beneath it and wrapped around the butt of my 9 millimeter.

All night long, my head has been buzzing with the memory of killing Lucius juxtaposed with the memory of Lucius cornering me in the parking garage. He's very much alive, and he fucking *knows*. He knows it was me. That knowledge alone is enough to ensure that I never sleep again. But what's worse than Lucius still drawing breath? I roll over and stare at the black envelope on the far corner of my dresser.

I have to open it. I should've done it yesterday, but I couldn't. Not when I barricaded myself into my loft apartment and sat up half the night with my gun pointed at the door.

But the boogeyman hadn't shown up, hadn't come banging on the door demanding I face him. Maybe Lucius doesn't know where I am.

I laugh in the quiet room. Not Lucius. He knows exactly where I am. He's probably already got a tail on me, and though I paid a lot of money to hide my past, he'll find out the truth. Maybe he already has. When he does, he'll know why I'm here to destroy him, and I hope he knows just how much he fucking deserves it. If he doesn't, well …

"Then it's war." I sigh, the liquid courage from last night threatening me with a headache of epic proportions. War with the Vinemonts. With *him*. It's what I planned for—a surgical strike on their business followed by a full-on takeover. Then, instead of increasing profits and making shareholders happy, I'd run it into the ground. Break it apart like a faulty toy and set the pieces on fire. Warm my hands as they burn.

But now it won't be so easy. Not when Lucius knows exactly what sort of threat I am. One willing to kill him with a single bullet and never look back.

Shit, Evie. Come the fuck on. I know what I'm doing. Stalling.

The envelope waits while I keep thinking about Lucius. The same way I've been thinking about him for years. Only this time … this time I know what it feels like to have his hands on me. Those hands ended my brother's life without mercy, and I have no doubt that it's a sin against my family for me to have felt something in those moments when Lucius had pinned me against him. I wanted to feel only revulsion, not fear, and definitely not ... Not anything more. Maybe the Acquisition didn't just twist the participants, maybe it broke something in me, too. Because I was there, because I witnessed every bit of horror—maybe that's why I want things that don't make sense. Maybe that's why I want to kill Lucius. Not just to avenge my family, but because perhaps it will destroy that fucked-up part of me that wants to get closer to him.

Jesus. If I keep doing all this godforsaken thinking, I'll need a drink sooner rather than later.

Sitting up, I pull the gun from beneath my pillow and place it on my nightstand. The sun isn't up yet, and condensation from the muggy air has crept up my locked balcony doors overnight. I eye the envelope, but once again, I can't bring myself to open it.

Instead, I force myself into a hot shower, and then I get ready. No board meetings for the day, so I just put on a little mascara and swipe some bronzer across my cheekbones. Dressing in a business casual navy top with white linen pants, I return to my bedroom as the sun peaks over the downtown skyline. The Crescent City is waking up, and now I have no excuse.

Pushing my shoulders back, I stalk to the envelope and snatch it off the dresser. It's paper. Paper can't hurt me. Despite that sentiment, my fingers shake as I break the crimson wax seal and open it.

Perfect calligraphy meets my eyes, and I try to skim the words. Just a brief, confident brush of my gaze across the ink, and then I can toss it like a piece of junk mail. But, of course, that fails, so I slow down and start from the top.

Miss Witherington,

As 'Interim' Sovereign, I am pleased to welcome you back to Louisiana. We need good stock to replenish our ranks and continue the tradition set forth by our ancestors. The incident from the last Acquisition must never be repeated, and I am working to ensure that another Acquisition takes place at the earliest possible opportunity.

This is a rebuilding phase, one in which I intend to gather all who remain committed to the old ways. As necessitated by the unfortunate events of the last Acquisition, I am also tasked with protecting this age-old institution from all who might seek to destroy it. In that vein, any who refuse to respect our traditions are, unfortunately, part of the problem I've been appointed to solve.

I'm certain you'd prefer to be part of the solution, which is why I'm extending this invitation with the greatest of anticipation. As a Witherington, one whose brother competed admirably in the last Acquisition, you will be afforded a place of honor within our society.

Your formal induction is set for Saturday the 24th, 7pm sharp, at the Corrigan Residence in the Garden District during a masked affair, as is our custom.

And, though I'm confident this goes without saying, if you fail to attend, I will personally make it my task to visit you at your 12th floor home on Perdido Street (door code 4361) at my earliest opportunity.

Yours very truly,

Sovereign

I'm covered in a cold sweat, and I didn't realize I'd sat at the foot of my bed. I stare at the words, at the horror. The Acquisition isn't over. It can't be killed. The Vinemonts burnt it to nothing but ash, but it's still alive. Not a phoenix, nothing resplendent like that. More like a demon who fed on the flames and only grew stronger.

I shouldn't have come back here.

My hands are cold, so cold I can't feel them as I let the parchment slip through them and hit the floor.

I sit for a long time, nausea roiling in my gut. It was foolish of me to think it was over. Just because my brother was dead right along with all the rest of them, that doesn't mean that some didn't survive. Or, perhaps, a new crop has risen. The children who were too young to attend the Sovereign's crowning all those years ago, or the ones off at college or overseas who didn't get caught up in the inferno.

After a while, I realize my phone's been buzzing intermittently. I look at it. Half an hour has passed, all of it spent in memory or conjecture. Bathed in cold sweat and wrapped in fear.

I swipe to answer the call. "Yeah?"

"Evelyn, are you all right?" It's Linton.

"Of course. Why?"

He clucks his tongue. "I don't know. When you answered, you just sounded..."

Like someone walked over my grave? "I'm fine. What's going on?"

"Craig Rasmussen called me first thing this morning."

That perks me up a little. Rasmussen is an influential board member for Magnolia. "What'd he say?"

"He wants to know if you'd like to meet for lunch."

"Yes. I mean, definitely. When?"

"Today."

Damn. I'll have to get myself together. No cracks in my armor, no dwelling on the hellish invitation that still lies at my feet.

"Evelyn?" he asks.

I realize I've been silent too long. "Set it up."

"He already has. Noon at Le Corbeau."

"Pick me up at 11:30?" I'll have to rethink my whole 'just mascara and bronzer' plan. Rasmussen will be expecting polished and perfect.

Linton clears his throat. "I'm afraid he made clear that he wanted to dine with you. Just you."

"Oh." I frown. "Is he up to something?"

"Likely." Linton sighs. "Don't overpromise. Don't tip your hand."

"I know." I stop just short of rolling my eyes. "But if

I can get him on our side, that's one step closer to taking over the board. A *big* step."

"Yes, but we can't be sure of his intentions ... or his ... *desires*. You know what I'm saying here."

Gross. "Rasmussen is what, 65?"

"Yes, 65, but not dead."

"Hell, if flirting gets me the leverage I need, I'm certainly not above it." I lie back on the bed and stare at the angular chandelier overhead. "I'll do anything to get Magnolia."

"Anything?" he asks delicately. "Let's hope it doesn't come to that."

"Go big or go home." I can't tell if this is empty bravado or if I'd actually sleep with Rasmussen if it meant winning Magnolia. After all, I already killed a man—at least I thought I did. What's a little disgusting sex? Still, I shiver.

"Be careful, Evelyn. I know how badly you want this, but you need to be able to walk away if that's what's best for you."

"I know what's best for me." I cut off that discussion. I don't need a father, and I certainly don't need Linton interfering with my plans.

We talk strategy for a few moments then hang up. I know what I need to do, and this opening couldn't have come at a better time. It's a new focus, a new place for me to spend my energy. Not the letter. The letter goes on the back burner. It's just an invitation.

I sit up and swipe the letter off the floor, then open

my dresser drawer and drop it in. Out of sight. In the dark.

If that beautifully-lettered paper is in there, hidden away, it can't hurt me...

That's likely the first of many lies I'll tell today.

11

LUCIUS

*L*e Corbeau is packed, diners at every table as the wait staff bustles about with dishes. I sit at a table near the kitchen, my back to the wall. From here I can see everyone and everything.

When Evelyn walks in, I take in every bit of her. The white sundress, pale blue pumps, and the way she's done her blonde hair. Breathtaking. I'm not the only one who stares. But I'm the only one who knows that beautiful exterior hides a tantalizing enigma.

She follows the maître d through the crowded room, but stops hard when she sees me sitting at the table. "Where's Rasmussen?"

"My apologies, Ms. Delacroix, but he couldn't make it."

"What did you do?" Her eyes narrow as her cheeks turn a high crimson.

"We had a chat, and he decided his time was better

spent elsewhere. So, I went ahead and took his reservation. You don't mind having lunch with me, do you?"

"I'd rather eat with a den of vipers," she hisses.

"Is that so, Evie?"

Her mouth opens, but no words come out. Yes, I know who she is now. Clever girl. My gaze strays to her hairline, to that false shade of blonde, and then to her eyes, a blue that doesn't fit. The last time I'd seen her was the night of the Sovereign ceremony, the night when the Acquisition came to a gruesome end. What a wonderful evening it was.

It was also the night when I killed her brother. No wonder it had been so easy for her to pull the trigger.

She snaps her mouth closed, her eyes burning. "It doesn't matter that you know my old name."

"Does it matter that you shot me in the chest, and I have the entire incident on 4k video that I could easily hand over to the police? You were, of course, wearing a mask, but my cameras stretch quite far across my property and onto my neighbor's. Including along the gravel road by the bayou, the one where you returned to your car and removed your mask. HD video is quite detailed, I find." I must admit I love torturing her like this. Every word from my mouth is a lie. I have no video of her, and I wouldn't trust the police with my luggage, much less my life. But the words still seem to hit her hard, because the color drains from her face.

"Please, Evie. Sit down." I gesture to the chair across from me.

I don't know why she complies. Not exactly. But I suspect that if she didn't, her knees might give out on her.

I unfold her napkin and drape it across her lap. "I've taken the liberty of ordering for you. I'll get you a Shirley Temple from the bar."

That gets her to look at me. "I'll have a gin and tonic. Double."

It seems I'm not the only one with a rotten liver, according to Teddy. Our server arrives after I send him a glance, and I order her drink.

Once he's gone again, I sip my own cocktail and study my enemy. I can imagine her mind is a whirlwind of worry and fear right now. Terror, maybe. She's probably scared that I—

"I hate your fucking guts." Her voice is low, almost feral. "This changes nothing. I'm still going to take Magnolia from you."

I didn't think I could get shocked anymore. I was wrong. This woman—fuck, the brass balls she has. She wants me dead, and I want to know what she tastes like.

"There's no chance of that, darlin'. If you'll remember your history, you'll know that the Vinemonts always come out *on top*."

Her nostrils flare as I emphasize the last two words. Interesting. Maybe little Evie has grown into a woman who wants things she shouldn't. Like, for example, the man who killed her brother in cold blood. In my defense, Red Witherington was a murderous bastard who would've robbed, killed, and raped his way through this world if I'd left him alive. Still, blood is blood. He was hers. And his blood is on my hands.

"I don't care what fairy tales you and your vicious brothers tell yourselves about your family name. I know who you are and what you're capable of."

"You do?" I sip my drink as hers arrives. "You know all the men I've killed? The ways I did it? How much I enjoyed it?"

"I saw you, Lucius." She grips her drink, her knuckles going white.

Our food arrives, and she glares at me the entire time our servers lay out a feast before us.

Once they're gone, she continues, "I saw what you did to Red. I saw the glee in your evil fucking face as you sank the knife into his heart while I begged you not to."

I shrug.

Her eyes flash, and she starts to rise.

I reach out and grab her by the hair, keeping her in her seat.

She lets out a scream, and then she looks around. Her voice, a pitch higher and feigning desperation: "Someone, please, help!"

The restaurant doesn't react. Everyone continues eating, drinking, talking—though perhaps it's a little more subdued than before.

I pull her closer to me, leaning her from her chair

so far that she has to rely on my hold in her hair to keep herself upright. "No one's going to help you, Evie." I duck my head and run my lips across her throat.

She gasps. "Help! Please!"

Licking the fluttering vein along her neck, I get a faint taste of her, of the sweet and salty. Fear and desire. Fuck, I want so much more.

With a push, I release her, and she rocks back into her chair.

"Out," I say quietly.

The entire restaurant stops. Each person rises, and everyone files out the front door as Evie watches, her eyes huge. Even the wait staff and the kitchen workers leave.

She looks around, eyes wide and confused, then slowly returns her gaze to the only other person here.

"Would you like to scream some more? I quite enjoyed it." I take my fork and knife and begin cutting into my rare filet as if nothing is amiss.

"You fucking bastard. You set all this up. Every bit of it."

I can't tell if she's in fear or awe. Maybe some of both.

"Did it turn you on when I pulled your hair?" I take a bite of steak, the meatiness melting on my tongue.

"Did it turn you on when I shot you in your black heart?" she fires back.

I smirk. "Actually—" I fork a piece of filet and offer it to her.

She ignores it.

"Actually, yes, Evie. It did." I eat the piece she wouldn't touch. "Now, tell me. Did you choose to wear that virginal little sundress so you could seduce a member of the board?" I glance down at her hard nipples as they press against the fabric. Fuck, I could cut my tongue on those, and I sure as hell want to try and find out. "Did you want him to take you to the bathroom, yank down those panties and fuck you against the wall?" I chew slowly as she glares at me.

"What makes you think I wore panties?"

I stop chewing. My mouth waters, but not for steak.

She smirks right back at me. "Like I said. It doesn't matter if you know who I am. I'm going to take what's yours, and once I have it, I'm going to tear it apart."

"All because I stabbed Red in the heart with a smile on my face?"

She tenses, her gaze darting to the steak knife on her side of the table.

"Do it." I put my knife down and gesture toward hers. "I want to see if you can."

"You want to see if I can kill you?" She takes the knife in her palm. "I already did it once. What makes you think I can't do it again?"

"Come and get me, little Evie." I spread my arms wide, and I don't miss the way she takes in my broad chest, the way her gaze follows my throat all the way to my lips, and then up to my eyes. She wants me. That little hair-pulling incident was just a tease. Soon enough, I'll be deep inside her, hurting her while she comes on my cock.

"It was kind of you to get rid of all the witnesses." She stands, her body lithe, as if she knows just what to do with the knife in her palm.

"Anything for you, little Evie." I raise my glass to her and down the rest of my whisky.

As I do, she lunges, the knife aimed right for my chest.

12

EVIE

All my force goes into burying the knife into Lucius. I want him to hurt the way I hurt when I think about what he did to Red. I want him to feel the same agony as the knife cuts through his life, slices open his heart, and leaves him to bleed out.

I'm almost there when he grabs my wrist. Whipping me away from him, he comes up behind me and grabs me with his other arm. With a roughness that jars through me, loosening all the parts that I've kept tightly wrapped over the last five years, he slams me onto the nearest table face down.

He leans over me, his body hard and heavy, forcing me down. And then I feel his length pressing against my ass.

I whimper. I shouldn't have, because he runs his teeth along my ear.

"Was that an invitation?" He moves his hips against me, showing me just how thick and hard he is.

"You're a fucking monster."

"You're the one who keeps trying to commit murder. How am I the bad guy in this scenario?" He grabs my hair and pulls it so my cheek is flat against the table. "I hate that you dyed your hair. Red suits you. And those contacts—I remember your big brown eyes. The way you used to look at me."

"Like I hated you?"

"Like you wanted to be underneath me. The way you are right now." His warm breath on my neck sends goose bumps racing across my skin.

"I was a foolish little girl."

"And now you're a foolish woman." He kicks my ankles, knocking my legs apart and pressing his cock against my hot core. "Bent over a table and about to be fucked by the man you hate the most."

"Get off me." I buck.

He laughs in my ear. "Are you sure that's what you want?"

"I hate you." Tears burn in my eyes.

"That's not what your cunt is telling me." He presses against me again, sending a shiver of need through me. "No panties, right?" Releasing my hair, he slides his fingers up my thigh.

"Stop." I try to buck him again.

"I will." He pauses, his fingers resting against my

upper thigh. "But I need you to answer some questions."

"Yes, you're a fucking prick. There. Question answered. Now get off me."

He laughs low and throaty, then nips at my neck. "No, darlin', that's not the question. What I want to know is, are you with them?"

"With who?" I don't know why I ask the question, why I bait the fucking bear on my back.

"Don't play coy." His fingers drift higher. "You know who I'm talking about, Evie."

"I don't." I do.

"If you don't come clean, I'm afraid I'm going to have to finger-fuck you." His fingers slide higher. "Rest assured, this will hurt me more than it hurts you, little Evie."

I bite back a moan. How long has it been since anyone's touched me? Even like this—maybe *because* it's like this, because I'm completely broken on the inside—I want to be touched. By him. By the devil.

"No!" I yell, in an effort to save myself, to somehow untwist my soul from around this warped man. "No, I'm not with them."

His fingers stop again, but they're so close to my pussy that I know he has to feel how wet I am. "Have they contacted you?"

The black envelope flashes in my mind.

"No."

His fingers trace circles on my burning skin. "Are

you certain? I'd hate for you to lie to me. That would require some punishment. Have you ever had four fingers inside you? Would that stretch your sweet little cunt terribly? I bet it would. But I bet you'd beg me to stop using my fingers and use my cock instead."

"I'm not lying! Now let me go!" I make one last plea for my sanity, for my soul.

"We could've had so much fun, Evie. I know how much you wanted it." He sighs and bites my ear before backing away.

I whirl and feint with my left. He buys it, so when I land a vicious right on his chest—in the same spot where my bullet should've killed him—he gives me a surprised look and takes a step back.

"Ow." He touches his chest and glares at me.

"Magnolia is mine." I yank my bag from beneath the table and keep him in my sights. "Don't you *ever* touch me again."

"Or what, Evie?" He advances with sure steps even though I know his chest must be throbbing. "You'll kill me again?"

I back away, knocking over a chair and another table. "I'll put you down for good, Lucius."

"Why? We could have so much fun together." He keeps coming. "I know who you are now. Not Evie Witherington. That doesn't matter. What matters is that you like what I do to you." His ocean blue eyes threaten to swallow me whole. "And you want more."

"Stay the fuck away from me!" I bump into the bar, then turn to run.

He grabs me, pulling my back to his chest and splaying his palm on my stomach. His lips to my ear send a shudder of desire through me.

"Hate me all you want. After all, I killed your brother, and I'd do it again."

"I fucking loathe you!" I scream so loud my throat goes ragged. I struggle, but he holds me tight.

His voice is still low. "Come after Magnolia. Come after me. Do your fucking worst, Evie. I deserve it and more. But I only want you to promise me one thing."

That caress of his voice, the feel of his arms around me—it's like a snake staring into my eyes, lulling me into a place of calm desperation.

"What?" I breathe out.

"When you need someone to take care of this—" He slides his hand down and cups my pussy through my dress. "You come to me. Take all that hate and rage out on me, little Evie, and I will reward you with all the pain and pleasure you can stand, and some you can't."

"You're sick," I spit the words, but I don't know if I'm talking to him or myself.

"And you're mine," he says darkly before letting me go.

I bolt out the front door of the restaurant and into the light. It feels like I've been locked inside hell with the devil for an eternity, like the entire world shifted on its axis. But out here, the sun still shines and jazz wafts through the air like always.

When I'm two blocks away and getting strange stares, I stop running. And when I've gone another block, I look behind me.

Lucius is there. Standing outside the restaurant and staring at me.

I can't tell his expression from this distance, but the hairs on the nape of my neck stand on end.

I want to cry, to scream, to run back to him and let him bend me over that table again, but this time I want him to take and take and take. Until there's nothing left of me. No more hurt, no more vengeance, nothing except Evie Witherington, a hopeful girl with her life ahead of her.

But that's not possible. Not for me or for him.

"You all right, miss?" A server from a patio restaurant looks at me curiously. I didn't notice her standing there at all.

"I-I'm fine. Thanks."

"Okay." She doesn't seem convinced, but she has too many diners to waste time on me, so she moves along.

When I look back for Lucius, he's gone.

13

LUCIUS

"Where have you been?" Teddy wolfs down a protein bar as I walk into the penthouse. "You're not a morning person."

"I had a lunch date."

He gives me a narrow look. "With who?"

"Mind your business." I throw myself down onto the couch, memories of Evie pirouetting through my head.

"Sin said that woman is actually Evie Witherington. That true?" He grabs another vitamin water. The kid is always at the hospital. I'm surprised he's spending any of his precious doctor minutes talking to me.

"Yep." I shrug. "I think she's mad at me."

Teddy guffaws. "You *think*?"

"Can't be too sure, especially since I also think she's desperate to fuck me."

He chokes on his swig of vitamin bullshit. "What?"

I nod at him. "Look at me, Teddy." I gesture toward my body. "Of *course* she wants to fuck me. Don't act surprised. But there's more to it."

"More to it? Like the fact you killed her brother *right in front of her*? Maybe that part? Or maybe the fact we burned a house down on her parents."

"No, not that shit. I'm talking about the slavery cosplayers."

"She's part of the Acquisition?" He swipes a hand through the air. "Wait. Hang on. You had lunch with *her*?"

"No. Well, yes I had lunch with her. No, I don't think she's part of it. Not yet, anyway." I think back to how she'd reacted when I'd asked her about it. "I think she hates them. Or, at the very least, wants nothing to do with them."

"And?" He grabs his backpack.

"And I think they've contacted her. I think they want her to be one of their new members, especially given her brother's place in the last Acquisition. They're trying to bring it all back, and if they can find even a twig of one of the old family trees, they're going to shake it."

"Did she tell you that?"

"No." I arch a brow. "She lied to me about it."

"Don't ..." He sighs. "Don't do anything to her, okay?"

Sweet Teddy. He's the only member of our fucked-up family who's ever had a care for others. Empathy. It's a strange concept, one I'm not familiar with on any real level, but I can see it shining in his eyes. Even though he was very nearly killed by the dregs of that secret society of craven bastards, he still sees good in people. He still wants to help others.

I don't get it. I never will.

"Why, little brother, whatever could you mean?"

"You know what I mean." He heads for the door, then pauses. "She's a victim, too, you know? A victim of the whole damn thing. None of it was her fault. She was just a kid with a brother who—"

"—was a fucking sociopath. I put him down like the dog he was."

"And I don't fault you for that. I never have." He shoulders his backpack. "Red was garbage. Evie isn't. You spared her. Don't you remember? When you killed Red, you could've taken her, too. Ended it right then and there. You didn't."

I shrug. "We'd given our word."

He gives me a knowing look. "Sin gave *his* word. You never promised to spare her. But you did anyway. Have you ever thought about why?"

"I don't make a habit of thinking about anything for too long. If I did, I could get ideas. And no one wants that." I smirk at him.

"Don't hurt her." He opens the door and slams it behind him.

"But what if she *wants* me to hurt her?" I ask the empty penthouse.

After pouring myself a generous drink, I grab my laptop and check over the newest leads on my darling little firebrand. She's an imposter, but a good one. None of my people have been able to track down her foreign accounts, but her domestic holdings are a nice chunk of change. I flip through bits of information, most of it glancing or unimportant. Until I find one item someone scavenged from her emails that piques my interest.

An old offer letter to my brother and signed by "*Mr. E. Weathers*" for a piece of property in the parish. I scroll through the document, and even though she styles herself as a man, I recognize her touch. She wants a particular stretch of fifty acres near the river, and she's offered a ridiculous sum for it.

I flip over to my secure server and do a search on the Vinemont holdings. Ah. She's trying to buy back a piece of her family's estate. One it just so happens I own. I grin at the screen. It seems I have several things little Evie wants.

Closing my eyes, I see her bent over that table, her dress hiked up, her body arching. She wants me. And she fucking *hates* that she wants me. I lean back in my chair and relish the memory of her. She knows who I am, what I've done—and yet. *And yet*. It's twisted as fuck, but it turns me on even more to know she wants my cock almost as much as she wants me dead.

I start to unbuckle my belt for a one-handed stroll down memory lane with Evie when my phone pings with an incoming text. I groan and check it.

Sin: Did you handle it?

Lucius: I was about to, but you interrupted.

Sin: This isn't a game. I need to know that you have Evie under control.

Lucius: I have her. Go play house with your little family. Let me do what I do best.

Sin: Stand around with your dick in your hand?

Lucius: Fuck you.

Sin: Stella says dinner tonight at seven.

Lucius: No. I need to stay in the city. I can't make it tonight.

Sin: It's your funeral.

I toss my phone beside me. Fuck. Dealing with Sin is one thing. Having to catch hell from his wife is something entirely different.

After finishing my glass, I get up and pack all my shit. Looks like I'll be spending the night at my place. It's probably a good idea anyway since I haven't disposed of Leonard yet. No rest for the wicked and all that.

I start to head out, leaving the city for the swampy countryside, but my car seems to guide itself around the French Quarter and right to the high-rise where Evie is staying. I can't see her from the street of course. She's high above me. What is she doing up there? I know she's home. The tail I put on her apprizes me of every move my little vixen makes.

Is she scared? Turned on? Both? I have half a mind to park and go on up to her floor. To ring her doorbell, and if she opens for me, charge in and give her what she needs. What *I* need. I want her more than I should. My hand goes to the bruise again, the spot where she almost pierced my black heart.

And then I drive on. Because Evie is just one of many problems I have on my plate. Even so, she's the one that occupies me for the entire drive back to my home parish and the Vinemont estate. The house I grew up in still stands at the end of a long row of oaks. It's traditional, beautiful, and full of ghosts.

"Uncle Lucius!" Little Teddy flings open the large front door and jumps into my arms the moment I make it to the top step.

I catch him and carry him inside. "You're heavier than last time."

"I'm a big boy now," he says proudly. "Mommy said I can go shooting with her tomorrow."

"Is that so?" I kiss his blond head and put him on his feet. "Bow or gun?"

"Both." He grins. The eyes of his mother, the cleverness of his father, and even a touch of innocence from his namesake, my brother Teddy.

Toddler chatter comes from down the hall, the twins Rebecca and Renee having a spirited conversation.

This house was never filled with sounds like this when I was young. So much life and love and joy in these formerly-dreary halls. It's almost like a completely different house, but then again... I stop and look at the portrait of my mother that graces the back of the foyer. This house may have changed, but it still has its echoes of pain.

"Food's ready!" Stella strides down the hall with a platter of barbecued chicken and delivers it into the dining room.

My stomach growls. I suppose I hadn't had much for lunch. No time for it, what with all the threatening and dry-humping I did with Evie. There my mind goes again, back to that slip of a woman with a heart full of anger.

"Do you see this?" Stella asks Sin.

"I see you." He reaches for her and pulls her into his lap at the table.

She sighs and leans against him. "No, I mean your brother. He's got stars in his eyes."

"Not at all." I take my usual seat at the table and blow a kiss to the twins. They giggle and babble to each other.

Sin strokes his hand along Stella's arm, and then across her chest where her vine tattoos snake from beneath her top.

"Gross." Teddy bounds in and plops down next to me.

"Agreed." I take his plate and fill it up for him.

"It's her, isn't it?" Sin adopts his usual glower as Stella disentangles from his lap and starts cutting up food for the twins. "She's gotten into your head."

"She's gotten to his head all right." Stella gives a very pointed glance at the table, right above my crotch.

"Yes, I want to get to know her better." I shrug. "That's smart. Keep your enemies closer and all that."

"Mmmhmm." Sin isn't convinced. He never is. "Do you have any more information on her? What happened at lunch?"

I opt to leave out the parts about me almost impaling her with my cock and, instead, tell him that she's dead serious about taking Magnolia. "Also, she lied about—" I glance at Teddy who has mashed potatoes smeared on the side of his mouth. "*Them.*"

"She's with them?" Sin's grip on his silverware tightens almost imperceptibly.

"No." If I had said yes, Evie wouldn't have lasted the week. We don't take chances with anyone who supports the Acquisition.

"Then why did she lie?" Stella wipes Teddy's mouth and kisses the top of his head. "Use your napkin."

"I don't know, but I have a gut feeling she's not interested in whatever they're offering her. I'll need to do some more digging. With the business, though, she's obviously trying to play games with me."

"Shooting you was a game?" Stella wrinkles her nose.

"Someone shot you?" Teddy's eyes widen.

"Just a Nerf gun. Don't worry."

"He's lying to protect you." Stella shakes her head. "I can't do that. You need to know the threats. It was a real gun, Teddy." She holds his gaze. "Remember those people who tried to take you?"

He swallows hard and nods.

"Never let your guard down. Lucius is a lesson in that. He took a bullet because we have enemies, ones that want to hurt us more than they want anything else in this world. That's why we always protect ourselves and our family. Understand?"

"Yes ma'am. I'm ready." He straightens, his little chest puffing out.

"We'll see about that tomorrow." She relaxes a little. Stella is so different from the person she was when she first set foot into the Vinemont world. In fact, the iron in her spine reminds me a little bit of ... my mother. I can only hope the similarities end there.

I want to tell her to go easy, that he's only six, that we defeated the devils who tried to kill us all. But I can't. She's right. The sooner Teddy realizes it, the better for him. Even so, we don't talk about the Acquisition in front of him. No more than mentions of "them" and knowing looks. He's still a child, and those boogeymen can stay hidden in the dark a little longer.

"Why did someone shoot you?" he asks.

I take a bite of my chicken and chew slowly, then say, "Probably because she was scared."

"Scared of you?" He swigs his milk. "Good."

"Not good." Sin chimes in. "We never want people to know we're a threat until it's too late for them. But that's a lesson for another day." He flicks his gaze to me. "Now, about Magnolia. What's your plan to handle the shareholders?"

I take a swallow of wine. "The usual." The usual in Vinemont terms includes a bevy of tactics including, first and foremost, intimidation. Our reputations should be enough to keep the shareholders in line. If that's not the case, I'll give each of them personal demonstrations of what happens when someone crosses us.

Sin nods. "I'll keep an eye on the proxy requests. If she starts racking them up, we'll have to go harder against her."

"Evie sounds tricky. If she's anything like her brother ... Don't underestimate her." Stella gives Renee a scoop of apple sauce.

"She's not like Red. But she's definitely changed, hardened I guess."

"Sounds to me like she chose to survive," Stella says. "I can't fault her for that. But if she tries to hurt my family, I won't show her any mercy."

Sin reaches out and caresses Stella's face. "I knew there was a reason I married you."

"You married up." She nips at his fingers.

Teddy and I share an exasperated glance.

My phone buzzes, and I pull it out of my pocket for

a quick look. What I see must telegraph to my face, because Sin asks warily, "What?"

I wipe my mouth and stand. "Thanks for the dinner. I've got to head out."

"Why?" Stella's eyebrows rise, suspicion in her eyes.

I turn the phone around to show her the screen of my surveillance app.

"There's a ghost in my woods." My blood seems to roar louder in my veins at the thought of seeing Evie again. "I think I'll go home and let her spook me."

14

EVIE

I shouldn't have come back here. Not when I have plenty of work to do with taking over Magnolia. Not to mention that goddamn black envelope. The invitation is for this Saturday—two days away. But I can't seem to focus. Not on work, not on anything. Only ... him. The way he touched me, the things he said. I can't get them out of my mind.

I should've just rubbed one out in my tub, but I didn't. Instead, I found myself driving back to the parish where I grew up. Back to the house where I killed a man. Or at least I thought I did. This land is cursed. It has to be. Sometimes when I'd come out here, I'd talk to Red. After all, he died not fifty yards from where I'm standing.

He doesn't talk back, though. I can't say I feel him, either. I must not be spiritual enough, or maybe he simply isn't here. Maybe he's in a better place. But I know that thought is a lie the second I have it.

I duck under a branch and push away those memories. The screams. The fire. The blood. They're part of me now, the reason I'm a charred soul inside a young woman's body. Burned and blistered, the wounds still raw.

Lucius's house is dark, the angular corners overcoming the night with shadows of their own. The wind sighs through the trees overhead, a breeze that gives little respite from the heat. I'm not wearing a mask this time. He already knows who I am. Still, it's not like I'm going to knock on his door and announce myself, so I'm wearing black from head to toe. Besides, the long sleeves and pants keep the mosquitoes at bay.

Minutes tick by as I simply wait. For what? I'm not sure. Maybe for Red. Maybe for Lucius. Maybe for some semblance of sense that will send me back to my car and to my apartment in New Orleans.

"Are you here, Red?" I whisper to the dark. "I miss you."

The silence doesn't respond. Not a falling star or a whistling wind. Just silence and stillness. I wait for long moments. Time passes slowly and fails to change the fact that I'm alone, and I'll always *be* alone.

Yes, this land is cursed. Just like my family name. I can't escape who I am, but I can stop coming here, stop looking for a ghost or the devil who killed him.

I turn to leave and stop. My heart sinks low into my

gut, and acid rises in my throat. I almost let out a scream, but I manage to swallow it down.

"Do you just stand out here and stare?" Lucius has his arms crossed over his chest as he leans casually against a pine tree. "Seems sort of strange, right? Are you a peeping Tammy?"

"How long have you been there?" I pat my pocket, the gun giving me at least a sliver of comfort.

He follows the movement, then smirks. "Going to shoot me again?"

"Maybe." I try to calm my breathing, try to make myself relax and focus.

"Didn't work the first time. What makes you think you can take me out now?"

"This time I'll shoot you in the face."

"You can't mean that. *This* face? This undeniably handsome face?" He tsks.

"What do you want?"

"That's a funny question coming from someone trespassing on *my* property."

"I'm not here for you."

"Lie." He steps forward, still far enough away for me to feel almost safe, almost as if I could get away.

I hate him so much. I can't even visit my brother's final resting place without Lucius stomping in like Godzilla. "I shouldn't have come here."

"That's the smartest thing you've said yet." He moves closer.

"Why did you buy the Oakman property? To gloat?"

"Something like that." Another step nearer to me. "To piss on their ashes. To celebrate their deaths."

"My parents were in that fire." I grit my teeth. "My whole family is dead because of yours."

"Is that what you tell yourself? That I'm the villain?" He cocks his head to the side. "That the Witheringtons were innocent bystanders? You think Red was—"

"Don't say his name!" The words burst out of me with explosive anger. I think it surprises me more than Lucius. That deep, unending well of hurt inside me yawns like the grave, open and oozing, poisoning my whole life. And Lucius is the reason it's there at all.

"You mean Red?" His smirk grows as he moves nearer. Like a shark scenting blood or a fighter pounding away at the one weak spot in his opponent, Lucius comes for me. "Red was a murderer. He killed and raped and hurt everyone he could, and you know it."

"Shut up."

"No." He's finally in front of me, close enough to touch.

I have to tilt my head back to meet his eyes. They're vicious, intense, the kind of eyes a foolish young girl could easily get lost in. But I'm not her anymore.

"Red was a menace, and I did you a favor by putting him d—"

My fist moves of its own accord. When it meets his jaw, he barely moves from the impact. My knuckles ricochet with pain up my arm as he moves so quickly, his touch light and then firm as he whips me around and wrenches my arm behind me. His other hand goes to my neck, his grip possessive, hot.

I should've shot him. I should've done so, so many things instead of ending up at his mercy all over again. God, I'm such a fool. A fatalistic little fool.

"Familiar, little Evie?" He pushes his erection against my backside.

"Get off me!" I struggle, but he pulls my arm up higher until the pain forces me to go still.

"Look out there, past my house, over to the right. See that line of oaks? Remember that?"

"Shut up!" I scream.

"That was the estate's grand driveway. And there at the end, that was the chateau. I remember when it was in flames, a beautiful sight." He presses his lips to my ear.

I shiver at his touch. "You murdered all those people."

"I'd do it again. All those people. Your family. Every last one of them, if it meant my family would be free. If it meant the fucking bullshit pageant of the Acquisition was never held again. You should be dead, Evie. You know that, right? Red lost. He *lost*. He didn't fight hard enough for you."

"He loved me!" I scream as hot tears well in my

eyes. "I don't care if he hurt people. I don't fucking care! He loved *me*! He protected *me*. He always did. He was all I had. He loved me, and you took him away from me." I can't stop the sob that bubbles up, and now I can see Red again, the look in his eyes when he died. The way his gaze held mine as Lucius took his life.

"I don't deny that, Evie. I know he loved you."

"Wh-what?" My eyes swim, blinding me until I can't see Lucius's house or the dark trees beyond. Maybe the ghosts are there now, flitting through the grass, only visible through tears of anguish.

"Red begged us—Sinclair and me—for your life. Even if he lost, he wanted you to survive. So, yes, I agree he loved you. But that doesn't mean he wasn't a monster." He loosens his grip on my arm but doesn't let go. "It doesn't mean I was wrong to kill him, Evie."

"You're the monster."

He sighs and holds onto me, his hand still at my throat, his thumb moving back and forth across my skin in a caress. "I have to agree with that, too. I know exactly who I am, Evie. Do you know who you are?"

"The woman who's going to take your empire and then your life." Even I can hear the shake in my voice.

"It doesn't have to be like this." His voice is a low rasp in my ear. "I can take away that hurt." He slides his hand from my neck to my chest. "I can make you feel so fucking good, Evie." When he cups my breast, my breath hitches.

"Stop." I grip his wrist, but he pulls my twisted arm up higher behind my back, forcing me to arch.

"Are you sure you want me to?" He twists my nipple through my shirt and bra, his fingers adept at their task.

I can't think, can't stand to feel so many emotions all at once. He's tearing me apart with nothing more than a touch, and I hate him for it.

"Let me go."

He sighs, then releases me.

I turn and back away from him. "This is never going to happen."

"It already is." He watches me, his gaze hungry.

"Stay away from me."

"No." He says it so simply.

I pull out my gun and train it on him, my hands shaking. "I mean it."

"Maybe you think you do." He shakes his head slowly. "But I can feel you, little Evie. Your body shivering for me. I know what you want from me, and it's not Magnolia. It's not an apology for Red—which you'll never get from me. You don't want any of those things, no matter how much you lie to yourself."

"Shut up."

"You want me."

"I want you dead."

His cocky smirk is infuriating. "No, you want me inside you."

"You're crazy."

"And you're wet."

I should pull the trigger. For my sanity. For my soul. I should end this devil with a bullet to the face just like I said.

"Wet, hot, wanting—I bet if I ran my finger down your pink slit, it'd slide right into your tight cunt, wouldn't it?"

His filthy words seem to have taken the breath from my lungs. What's worse is that it's true. I'm fucked up, so damaged that I confuse lust with loss, the wires irrevocably crossed.

"I hate you," I whisper in a trembling voice.

"Keep telling yourself that, darlin'. Now run along home, little Evie. I'll see you soon. And then we'll finish this dance you've started." He turns and starts whistling as he trudges across the lawn to his house.

I lower the gun, finally feeling like I can breathe again.

But then he stops.

I can't take my eyes off him as he turns to face me.

"Be careful in those woods, little Evie. They're dark and deep, and you'd never know someone was after you until they had you." He flexes his hands as he stares me down.

Goosebumps races across my skin, and I back away slowly. He doesn't move, doesn't blink, just watches me like a snake waiting to strike.

When I'm farther into the trees, I turn and run. He could be after me, his steps muffled by my own. He could be racing around to cut me off, to toy with me. Lucius is so cunning, so damn cold. So I run as hard as I can, saplings slapping at me and my ankles threatening to roll. I don't spare a glance behind me, not when it would cost me time. I run until I find the dirt road that leads me out of that cursed property.

My heart rampages, my lungs ache, and though I try to deny it to myself, I *burn* for the monster at my back.

15

LUCIUS

"Holy shit, Leonard, are you still alive?" I flip on the overhead bulb and splash through the water to him.

His nose and mouth are above the surface, but not by much. I grip his soggy shirt and yank him upright, water running off him like I just raised the Titanic.

He gasps in air, his bleary eyes blinking as he shivers.

"I guess we really are in a drought or something?" I look around at the water seeping into the basement. "Lucky you."

"Let me go," he croaks.

"Nope. But hey, I'll make you a deal. Tonight only, I'm feeling magnanimous." I'm not even lying to him. Finding Evie in my woods tonight has put me in a good mood, except for the massive case of blue balls she's given me.

"What do you want?"

"Give me the name of the new Sovereign, and I'll make it quick. How about that?" I reach behind me and pull a knife from the weapons arranged along the cinderblock wall. "Nearly painless. Way better than drowning in swamp water." I turn my head sharply to the left. "Whoa, is that a snake down here? Cottonmouth from the looks of it."

"Stop." He breaks instantly, his snotty tears and blubbering rising in a rapid crescendo. "Please, please let me go!"

"Not happening. Accept it." I stand and wait, letting the old fool get it out of his system. "Shouldn't we already be at the acceptance stage by now? Besides, why are you being loyal to those assholes anyway? You don't see them running in to rescue you, do you? It's not like they've made any effort to free you. Some friends you've got, I tell you what."

I let the silence linger for a while, nothing but the sounds of dripping water and the phantom *swish* of the snake in the water. Boring. Waiting isn't my forte. But I can pass a little time remembering Evie's face when I told her what I'd like to do with my finger. She had this perfect mix of horror and desire; I can't even think of a word for it. All I know is I want more.

I've read up on her, followed every step she's taken over the past five years. It's as if we're old friends, ones who keep up with each other here and there, ones who can strike up an easy conversation even if we haven't seen each other for years. I knew her in the past, and now I know her present iteration. A woman who wants blood to pay for blood. I can respect it.

Leonard shivers so violently he sends waves pulsing through the black water.

"Ah, fuck it. I guess you can just drown. Maybe that ol' cottonmouth will keep you company." I lift my foot so I can kick his chair over again.

"Wait!" He coughs, the sound like death rattling its sabre, and glares up at me. "You swear to me, if I tell you the new Sovereign, you'll end it quickly?"

I pull down the collar of my shirt and show him the vines tattooed and tangled over my heart. "On my word as a Vinemont."

He spits again. "Not worth shit."

Well, over you go, then. I start to kick.

"Beau Corrigan!" he screams.

"What the fuck is that?" I stop with my foot on the chair. "Some sort of hipster clothing line?"

"The new Sovereign. He's from the families. An eldest son. He'd been in a car accident and wasn't at the crowning ceremony. He survived."

I can't place the name right offhand, but I'll find him. "Not for long."

"He'll put you down like a dog." He bares his teeth. "You and your whole heretic family!"

I return his pure animal hatred with my own. "You're lucky I'm a man of my word." With a quick swipe, I open his throat.

He's silent now, his thick blood dispersing in the bog water around his feet.

Reaching over, I start the pump running and replace the knife. I'll handle the rest of him in the morning.

I trudge back to the stairs and leave my swamp boots at the top. Once I'm out of the dank basement, I close the secret door and lock it, then secure it all behind what appears to be nothing more than a paneled dining room wall.

I grab my phone from the table and text the name to Sin.

It rings within a few seconds.

"That's his name?" His voice is low. I can hear the twins in the background and Stella trying to read them a bedtime story.

"The new Sovereign."

"Leonard broke?"

"Cracked like a rotten egg. He's gone now." I sigh as I pour myself a drink. "Going to be kind of lonely around here without him."

"Can you be serious for one fucking second?"

"What? I *am* being serious." It's a big house, after all. So much space for just one man. But instead of a Leonard, maybe I should fill it with more attractive prey.

"And Evie?"

"She's gone. We had a little heart to heart about

how badly she wants to ride my dick. Went swimmingly."

"Lucius." He says my name with the same warning tone he's used since we were kids.

I respond with the same smartass tone *I've* used since we were kids. "I'll handle her."

"The way you handled Leonard?"

For some reason, I don't like the thought of that. In fact, I find it ... abhorrent. "No."

He sighs. "We protect the family, Lucius. That's it. If you start thinking with your dick, you're going to make mistakes. A lot of them. We can't afford that right now."

"I'm perfectly level-headed. Calm the fuck down." I drain my glass. "I'll handle the Magnolia dealings, and I'll put my team of miscreants on finding every scrap of information on Beau Corrigan."

"Dada!" one of the twins squeals.

"Coming, sweetheart." When he speaks to his children, he's almost a completely different man. Then again, perhaps that's the sort of man he would've been if it weren't for the Acquisition. As it is, he's cold and calculating, much like me. It's the only way we could survive.

"I'll look back through Mom's stuff. That last name is familiar. They're definitely players. I just don't know how big."

"Talk tomorrow." I end the call and settle back in my chair, my gaze on the woods.

Evie is long gone. She probably thinks she's safe and sound in her little apartment.

I pour another and lift my glass toward the window. "To you, my darling survivor."

It doesn't even burn on the way down, and I sit for a while longer, my thoughts moving along the lines of her body, through the curves of her mind, and into the deep ravines of her heart.

She loved her brother. That's the fact I keep returning to. She loved him, even though she *knew* he was a monster.

I swirl my bourbon and ponder that simple yet impossibly complex truth. And then I take the next step. The one that I've been holding my breath for from the moment she shot me in the heart.

If she already loved one monster, why not another?

16

EVIE

The Garden District boutique is small, unassuming, and only for the filthy rich denizens of this city.

I select a handful of gowns and sip Riesling as I try them on. My assistant zips me into them and looks at me with a critical eye.

The entire thing is a farce, and I'm nothing more than a child playing dress-up in my mom's fancy clothes. But I play the part. I have to. This is what the Sovereign expects me to do. And I know without a doubt they're watching my every move. So, I drink my white wine and try on dress after dress until I find one that fits the occasion.

"Classic, clean lines, and elegant on you. It accentuates your long neck and high bust and helps subdue the widening of your hips." Jeanette taps her finger on her lips.

We wouldn't want anyone being offended by my figure, now would we? I would laugh if I'd had more to drink. Or maybe if my heart wasn't sinking lower and lower with every second I get closer to the Acquisition affair. Just thinking about it makes my stomach churn, and I have to put my glass down.

"We have it in black or deep wine." Jeanette cuts me a sharp look when I start pulling the gown off.

"Allow me." She hurries behind me and strips me out of it.

"I'll take it in the wine color, please."

"Yes, ma'am. I'll take it to the seamstress myself. It will fit you like a glove." She squeezes out the door and closes it, and the moment she's gone I sink onto the white chaise along the back of the dressing room.

I shouldn't be here. I should be out meeting with shareholders and board members, putting the stranglehold on Magnolia. Instead, I'm just trying to keep it together. I knew taking Magnolia would be difficult, but I didn't plan on the rest of it. Not the Sovereign, and certainly not the way Lucius gets under my skin.

He was so untouchable, like a dream to me when I was young. Now, he's a shadow that I glimpse at the edge of my vision. He's there, watching and waiting. The moment I stumble, he won't be there to catch me. He'll be there to rip me apart.

"Fuck." I rub my temples.

"Such language from a lady of your breeding?" The door opens and the man from the elevator walks in.

I sit up and glance at my bag. My pistol is there.

"Don't get up for me, Evie." He closes and locks the door behind him. When his gaze slides down my body, I snatch the silk robe from the back of the chaise and drape it across myself.

"What do you want?" I lean back, as far away from him as I can get.

"Nothing really." He only has to take one step to be close to me. Too close.

Panic starts to rise inside me, my airway closing and my heart thrashing against my ribcage.

"Where were you last night?" He looms over me, his blond hair and sharp blue eyes a façade to cover the darkness inside.

"I don't answer to you." I stand and pull on my robe, then move to step around him.

He grabs my arms in a rough grip and holds me in front of him. "I asked you a question, Evie. Where were you last night?"

I'm trapped. He isn't going to let me go, and no one can help me. I have to get out of here.

He leans down until he's only inches away from my face. "Answer the question, Miss Witherington."

"I don't answer to you, asshole."

He smiles. It sends terror cascading down my spine.

"You know, Evie, I'd hate to think you were doing anything that could jeopardize your standing with the new Sovereign."

"What I do is my business." I say the words, and I know they come out sounding confident, but inside ... Inside is another story.

"That's where you're wrong. What you do is my business and the business of the Sovereign. If he were to suspect that you were on pleasant terms with a certain member of the Vinemont family." He grimaces a little when he says the name. "That would cause a problem. I'm here to help you avoid those problems."

"Good thing I don't need your help."

His jaw tightens, and he pushes me back until I'm against the wall.

Fight or flight is having a hell of a disagreement in my gut.

"You should be careful, Evie. Tomorrow night is important for you, for the future of our world. And while the Sovereign is pleased at your efforts to take Magnolia from that vile family of reprobates, he would hate to hear that you've grown fond of any of them." His gaze slips to my lips. "*I* would hate to hear it too."

I feel a tickle of vomit at the back of my throat.

"You understand that, don't you, Evie?" He squeezes my arms even tighter and pins me with his big body.

"What part of me running Magnolia into the ground are you missing?" I can barely get the words out under his crushing weight. "I hate them, all of them. They killed my brother."

"Lucius killed your brother," he corrects.

"I know what he did!" I try to shove him off me, but he's far too big, too strong, and too hellbent on making those facts abundantly clear to me.

"Then we're on the same page." He gives me a fake smile and finally backs off.

My arms ache from his grip, but I refuse to rub them when he's watching. I won't show this bastard any weakness. Not now. Not ever.

"You really should've chosen the black." He reaches up and touches my hair.

I try not to flinch but fail.

"Don't be afraid of me, Evie." He drops his palm to my cheek. "I don't want to have to hurt you. But that depends on you, doesn't it?"

Spoken like a true fucking sociopath.

"I'll be there tomorrow night. Is there anything else you'd like to discuss?" I practically spit the words at him. "I'm a busy woman."

"I'll pick you up at 6:30."

"No." I back away from his touch. "I don't need an escort."

His jaw tightens again, and I can feel his anger like an electrical charge. I don't know who he is or why he's the one they chose to come for me, but they underestimated me. I won't be cowed by some crew cut psycho with anger management issues.

"Now, I'd like to continue my day. If you'd please see yourself out." I turn my back on him, even though every instinct inside me screams not to do it. But that's why I *have* to do it. It's a power move.

He's silent as I drop the robe and pull on my top, then reach for my skirt.

"Did you miss the part where I dismissed you?" I fasten the skirt and turn to find him glaring at me, his eyes glossy.

Holding my head high, I reach for my bag. For safety. For my loaded gun.

He smiles slowly in that same creepy way of his. "I like your spirit, Evie. I really do." He steps to me again, his hand going to my throat. "But if you keep pushing me like this, I don't think you're going to like the outcome."

"If you don't take your hands off me, neither are you." I press the barrel of my pistol against his ribs.

He glances down, then slowly returns his gaze to me.

"Now get your hands *off*," I hiss.

He releases my throat and backs up a pace. "Be ready. I'll be at your door at 6:30." That crackling rage inside him is roaring, but he tamps it down when my pistol is aimed at his chest. Without another word, he turns and leaves the fitting room.

As soon as the door closes, I jump over to it and turn the lock. My legs give way, and I stumble back to the chaise.

I refuse to let myself cry, and I wipe two errant tears from my cheeks and straighten my clothes. With another deep breath, I inspect my arms. The skin is already starting to bruise lightly. Pale yellow imprints of meaty hands.

I pull on my cream jacket and try not to scream. I'm trapped, backed into a corner with no way out.

There's nothing I can do to avoid tomorrow night, but I'll be damned if I let them terrorize me like this. I won't break. I won't fucking break. Not for them. Not for anyone. All I have to do is convince the girl who lives in my heart—the same girl who lost everything she ever loved five years ago—that those words are true. That I'm strong enough to survive this. I have to be.

Jeanette never reappears, so I slip out of the boutique and into the muggy New Orleans morning. She'll have the dress delivered on time; I have no doubt.

Once I'm in my car, I take deep breaths and try to fight the exhaustion I feel from the ebbing adrenaline rush. But I don't take a break, don't spend another second on it. Driving through the streets, I force it out of my mind. I've gotten pretty good at that over the years. Even so, my thoughts turn in an even worse direction. Lucius. When he has his hands on me, it's nothing like this. I should feel the same sort of revulsion, the same sort of violation, but I don't. How can it be so different? But that begs the question of why I'm such a twisted mess, and I can't get mired in that right now.

My next appointment is only a mile and a half away, the home of another board member. Mr. Angles is one of the few who have ever gone against Lucius's wishes. He's likely the most independent member of the board, but that doesn't mean I can get him on my team. It's going to take work.

I park and shake off the phantom sensation of that brute's hands on me. I push it down deep and lock it up. It can crop up later, sometime when I'm alone, when I can be vulnerable. But not here. Not today.

Pulling up out front of a sprawling Victorian mansion, I park and step from the car.

I'm halfway up the steps to the wrought iron fence when I see a familiar shape on the front porch. As if my day wasn't already a dumpster fire.

I almost miss the next step but catch myself.

Lucius waves from his spot on the swing, and Arlo Angles sips his iced tea on the sunny porch. Lucius's filthy words from last night float through my mind, and a shiver runs through me. Shame quickly colors over those thoughts. I shake it off and focus on winning, on beating Lucius at his own game.

"Mr. Angles. We have a meeting." I climb the four steps to the front porch, the wood planks a pearly white beneath my feet. The sun is oppressive today, the heat like a heavy touch.

"We do." He nods but doesn't make a move to stand and greet me.

Lucius, however, gets to his feet and comes over to me. "Would you like a drink?"

"I'd like a word with Mr. Angles in private." I narrow my eyes as he moves closer.

"Let's stick to things that are within the realm of possibility, shall we, darlin'?"

I've never met a man who needs a swift slap to the face as badly as Lucius. "You can't prevent me from speaking to the board of directors."

He moves past me to a drink cart set up against the shadiest part of the front wall. "Now, I can't say for sure, but you strike me as a mint julep girl."

"Are you listening to me?"

"Yes, darlin'. I hang on your every word," he says dryly. He drops some ice cubes into a glass and pours bourbon into a tumbler.

"Stop calling me darling, I don't want a drink, and I need to speak to Mr. Angles."

"Go ahead." He gestures with the tumbler in his hand. "Speak all you want."

"In *private*." I turn to Mr. Angles. "If we could perhaps go inside and sit down—"

"Heavy on the sugar, right?" Lucius holds up a packet with the Magnolia logo across it, then rips it open with his teeth and pours the sugar into the shaker. It's lewd and wrong, but he looks so good when he's doing awful things. He starts shaking the drink, his gaze never leaving mine.

I force my attention back to Mr. Angles. "Mr. Angles, please. I need to—"

"He's not going to talk to you." Lucius finishes shaking the drink and pours it into a glass.

"We set a meeting. You agreed to see me." I ignore Lucius and stare down at Arlo Angles. "Remember?"

"Berating him won't change it." Lucius adds some mint leaves and offers me the glass.

"What did you do to him?" I peer at the graying man who hasn't said a word. He won't meet my gaze, and he shifts uncomfortably in his seat.

"Do to him? Nothing." Lucius offers me the glass again.

I don't take it, and instead entreat Mr. Angles again. "Listen, it is burning hot out here. I think we'd be more comfortable if we moved this inside. Just you and me. I have some great plans for the future of Magnolia, and you would be doing your shareholders a great service by simply meeting with me about how to move the company forward into a more profitable future."

"Wow, you should do commercials." Lucius smirks.

I should've taken the drink, because right now would be the perfect time for me to throw it into his smug face. Instead, I walk to the sunny swing and sit down, then strip out of my jacket.

"Mr. Angles, we can have this conversation out here if that's the way it has to be. Okay, imagine a Magnolia that is—at minimum—thirty percent more profitable by year end. That's what your shareholders deserve, isn't it? You can continue to make—"

"What's that?" Lucius is towering over me. At least he's casting a shadow.

I keep going. "Now, the way to get to that profitability is to trim the fat and restructure the company from the top down. We keep the workers who—"

"Arlo, inside." Lucius's voice is almost a growl. "Now."

"We're having a conversation. Mr. Angles, I only need a little of your time." *Desperation has entered the chat.*

Arlo gets up, his knees popping, and hustles inside.

I stand to follow him and give Lucius an acid glare.

"Stop." He takes my elbow, but his touch is surprisingly gentle. "Who did this to you?" His gaze is on my upper arm.

Shit. I already forgot about the marks.

"No one." I reach for my jacket, but Lucius doesn't let go.

"Tell me who hurt you, Evie."

I meet his gaze. "Is that a joke? *You* hurt me."

"I'm not talking about five years ago. I'm talking about this." He runs his fingers down the bruised skin. "Tell me who did this to you. All I need is a name." His voice has that sinister quality that matches perfectly with his reputation and dark good looks. He's a killer, as sure as I'm standing here, Lucius has blood on his hands many times over.

"I don't have a name." I tell the truth; I don't know why. "And I can take care of myself."

"That's why you're sporting bruises like this?" He leans back to peer at my other arm. His gaze darkens even more when he sees the matching marks.

"Lucius, I don't need your help." I pull my arm from his grip. "Unless you want to go ahead and surrender the keys to Magnolia."

"Not happening." He takes my jacket from my hands and holds it out for me like a pleasant valet.

I give him a wary look, then slip my arms into it. He runs his hands along my shoulders and leaves them there until I step away from him.

"I'm glad we had this special time. Now, I need to speak to Mr. Angles." I march to the front door and turn the filigreed knob.

It's locked.

I ring the bell.

No one comes.

I can feel Lucius's eyes on me as I pull out my phone and dial Mr. Angles's number. Straight to voicemail.

Fuck.

I whirl on him. "What did you do? Threaten his firstborn?"

"Nothing so boring as that." He shrugs. "Everyone has their demons. I just know which ones to exploit."

"I'll get to him." I turn away from the door. "It doesn't matter what sort of bullshit you pull, I'm going to speak with each of the board members. And when I'm done with them, they're going to happily jettison you and your entire family from Magnolia."

He stares down at me for a moment, his face thoughtful. "How about we make a deal?"

"Now you're offering me a devil's bargain? Like I can trust you?" I want to laugh in his face, but at this point, I can't risk anything even close to that level of emotion. It could break me. Isn't it strange how strong feelings can call out their opposites? Laughter leads to tears or anger to desire.

Lucius reaches out to run his fingers along a lock of my hair. "I'll give you five minutes alone with Arlo if you tell me who hurt you."

I step back, needing distance between us. "Is this some sort of mind game?"

"Someone putting their hands on you isn't a game." He has that deadly tone again, the one that affects me in myriad ways, none of them good.

"In that case, you should keep your hands to yourself."

"I'm not just someone, Evie, and you know it." He moves closer, invading my space and making it his.

"It doesn't matter. I'll get to him sooner or later." I can't tell him what happened. Not just because I don't have a name, but because if he realizes I'm being dragged into the Acquisition, he might kill me. Something deep inside whispers that he'd never do that, but I can't trust that voice. It's the same one that pulled me out to his house last night. It's the voice of that foolish little girl who trusts everyone and gains nothing from it but pain.

"Ten minutes." He blocks my path back down the stairs. "Ten minutes alone with him to do your song and dance."

God knows I need this chance with Arlo Angles, but the cost is too high. "No."

"Fifteen." He searches my eyes with his gaze. "Fifteen minutes of uninterrupted saleswomanship. All I need is for you to tell me who. That's all I want from you."

"I don't believe you."

He gives me a wry look. "That last part may have been a lie, but the rest is true."

"Why do you even care? Have you forgotten this?" I poke his chest.

He grunts but doesn't move. "Evie, if you think a bullet can stop me from getting what I want, you have a lot to learn about me."

"I know enough." I push past him and hurry down the stairs. I have to get out of here. For some reason, the worry in his tone is breaking me apart bit by bit. The way he wants to know who hurt me—it's like a poison slowly spreading in my veins. If I don't get away from him, something inside me is going to burst. And when it does, I won't be able to hide anymore.

"Evie—"

"Leave me alone, Lucius!" I push through the wrought iron, rush down the stairs, and bolt to my car.

His hand comes down on the door, keeping it shut. He's beside me, his chest against my shoulder. I can smell his cologne, a light scent of pine and some sort of dark citrus. How can evil be molded into such an alluring man?

"Evie." He says my name softly this time, the way a lover would.

I can't trust myself to speak, not when the tears are already stinging behind my eyes.

"Let me help you. Please."

A million ways to cut him are on the tip of my tongue. Accusations. Curses. Insults. Everything I can think of and some extra venom on top. But I can't say any of them. Can't do anything except lean into him. Only for a moment. A small second where I'm not alone, where there's someone who can hold my burden if just for a fleeting flash of time.

He presses his lips to my hair. "Please, Evie."

And then I come to my senses, shove him away from me, get into my car, and leave him as fast as I can.

My tears don't wait for my apartment. I succumb only a few blocks away and have to park as I fall apart. At least I'm alone, I tell myself as I scream and beat the steering wheel, letting it all out.

But for the first time in years, being alone doesn't give me any solace.

17

LUCIUS

*E*vie takes a lunch meeting with her lawyer. Then she goes to Saks for a pair of heels and a cloak. After that, she takes a trip to the edge of the French Quarter and purchases a mask.

The tail I put on her has been quite detailed about all he sees as she goes about her day. I devour each word, hungry for more.

"Arlo is in line, I take it?" Sin stares out at the city from the Magnolia headquarters in the business district.

"Yes. His predilection for eighteen-year-old boys has caught up to him."

"Photos?" he asks.

"Video. He wouldn't want his wife to see it, much less the diocese where his son is a priest."

He stares out the window, his desk pristine. "Good. Who else will she try to pick off?"

"Unger is next, I'd bet."

"She contacted him yet?"

"No, which is not on par for her. She's veered off the path a bit today. Something else is preoccupying her. She bought a gown at a swank boutique, and now she's purchased a mask."

His eyebrow twitches. "Acquisition."

"They've contacted her." I saw the truth of it written on her body, in the bruises that she tried to hide. And when she leaned into me by the car, that one little hint of contact that seemed to me like a concession, an admission that she needs me. Not just anyone. *Me*.

He turns his gaze back to me. "You saw her at Arlo's house."

"Yes."

He simply stares in that creepy way of his. I'm immune to it, though. Have been for years. I'm not going to tell him what I learned or what I saw. Evie is my problem, my growing obsession. Hell, I haven't stopped thinking about her since she tried to kill me.

"If you fuck her, you're going to regret it."

"'If'?" I give him a patronizing look. "You mean *when*."

He pinches the bridge of his nose. "Why must you always try my patience?"

"I guess it's a middle child thing." I grab the glass reproduction of sugar cane from his desk and twirl it around in my hands.

"You're going to break that."

"I break everything eventually."

He sighs, low and belabored. "At least you know yourself."

"The most handsome Vinemont brother—yes, I certainly do." I've often wondered how many times Sin has pondered trying to kill me. He's the sort that likely would've strangled me in my sleep when we were kids, but somehow, I kept him entertained for long enough that he never tried it.

"Stella would disagree." Mischief glints in his eyes.

"Stella clearly has shit taste. After all, look who she married." I stand and place the glass cane back on his desk with a worrisome thud.

"I'm serious, Lucius." His usual glower returns. "The bad blood between our families isn't something you can fuck out of her. This goes too deep and too far back for it to ever be water under the bridge. Red meant more to her than a prick like him should have, but we can't change it. She'll always want revenge for it."

"I know."

"You say you know, but you still want to get your dick wet like a goddamn fool." He pauses and peers at me as he rises from his chair. "Unless..."

"Unless what?"

He approaches, scanning my face in the afternoon light. "Unless there's more there than an angry fuck."

I start to respond, but he throws his hands up. "Lucius!"

"What?"

"You can't be serious." He runs a hand through his hair. "She's our goddamn enemy."

"I know." I can't deny his claim, so I don't bother.

"Fucking hell." He stalks to the wall at the side of the room and opens the hidden bar.

"Make it a double." I meet him there and take the proffered drink.

"Once you fuck her, you'll be done with her." He nods, as if to himself. "That's what's going to happen. You've got the emotional maturity of a drunk toddler, so this will pass. What are you even thinking? You don't know her. You don't—"

"I know her." I finish my drink in one gulp. "Past and present. The future isn't quite so clear."

"If she knows you at all, she'll stay the fuck away." He's already given up trying to talk me out of it. I suppose that comes from years of experience. Once I find something I want, I don't stop until it's mine. Up until this point, though, that "something" has never been a person.

He sips his drink and turns to me. "What if she's with them? What then, Lucius? What if she chooses them over you? I mean, chances are good, right? She already *hates* you." He blinks as if he can't seem to wrap his mind around this conversation. "Jesus, this is a goddamn mess."

"She only *thinks* she hates me. She doesn't really hate me."

"Has she said anything—anything at all—to that effect?" He pours himself another drink. "Or has she said that she fucking hates you, with no caveats or asterisks?"

I mean, he has a point there. "Look, what she says and the way she reacts to me are two different things. After I cockblocked her at Arlo's place, she showed me something more. This isn't a one-sided thing. She knows there's something between us."

"Yeah, mutual hate." He shakes his head. "Let's play this scenario out, shall we? You somehow get between her legs, fuck her, and then what? Then what?"

"Then—"

"I'll tell you then what—then she stabs you in the fucking neck for killing her brother right in front of her five years ago. That's what."

"What a way to go, right?" I toast him and down the second glass.

He drops his glass onto the tray and rubs his eyes. "Why do I always have to be the level-headed one in this fucking zoo? Why?" He groans. "You need to stop thinking with your dick and focus on protecting Magnolia."

"I can multitask." This is the usual point in our conversations where we get into a fistfight. I shake out my arms. "Keep my face pretty. I've got a woman to woo."

"As much as you need your ass kicked, I have to go. Stella's friends are in town for the weekend."

"The Russian?" I love kicking that big oaf's ass.

"Yeah, but he's going to be busy training with Stella. She's trying to get stronger at krav maga."

"Scary thought."

He smiles—Stella's the only thing that's ever made him truly happy, and it fucking shows. "I can't wait to try her out, pin her down, and ..." His eyes go glossy as he pervs out in his imagination.

"Good chat." I turn and stride away from him.

"Watch your back, Lucius," he calls. "Evie's not some innocent princess anymore."

That's what I'm counting on. I pull my phone out as I head to my corner office. It's similar to Sin's but bigger. After all I'm the sugar magnate, and he's my second in command when it comes to the business.

Tyrone: Boss, she's got someone else watching her.

I frown at the text from the tail I put on Evie.

Lucius: Have you been made?

Tyrone: No.

Lucius: Keep an eye on them, too. If they leave, follow. I'll handle Evie tonight.

Tyrone: Will do.

Another tail. Hmm. Though I suspect Evie's made a handful of enemies during her rise to corporate power, I don't think any of them would be interested in following her around New Orleans. Nothing to gain from it.

However, there is one particular organization that I've no doubt wants to keep tabs on her. Those bruises on her arms are practically a calling card. My blood turns scorching at the thought of it. Some asshole thinks he can put his hands on my woman.

I stop at my window and watch as the sun sets. Sin was right about my lack of emotional maturity. Because as I stand here, I can't put into words what I'm feeling for that spitfire with the murderous intentions. I can't say love, because I've never truly known what that is. A sensation? A knowing? A what? What the hell is it?

I don't know, and I may never know. There's one word, though, that comes to me as I stare out at the fading light and bustling city below. One word that encompasses my world since Evie has been in it these past few days.

Want.

I *want*.

Her body, her mind, her passion. And maybe, yes, maybe her love. I don't deserve it, and I certainly don't understand it. But all the same, I *want* it, whatever it is.

My phone buzzes.

Tyrone: Evie returned from her afternoon meeting with the tail on her 6. Once she entered her building, the tail took off.

Lucius: Follow.

Tyrone. On it.

I glance at my laptop and the multitude of emails

that I'm certain await me. Contracts, counter-offers, reports on my sugar cane holdings in Cuba and South America. This empire was built on blood and sacrifice. My family depends on me, and I won't let them down. It's one of my few good traits, I suppose. Grabbing the computer, I stow it in my leather bag and head down to my car.

Watching Evie and working—piece of cake. Like I told Sin, I'm a multitasker. I'll stay in my car and keep an eye on her place until Tyrone returns.

Solid plan.

18
EVIE

It's late when I hear the knock at my door. But it's not as if I'm sleeping. With the Acquisition party tomorrow night, I can't focus on much besides my ever-growing dread. The knock shakes me out of it, and my skin crawls when I realize it's probably the man from earlier.

I can't deal with him again. How did he even get up here? What idiot would buzz him in? I don't move, just stare at the door as my panic mounts. Where's my gun? I glance at the empty bottle of Pinot and force myself to my feet. Unsteady, I lurch toward the couch and my bag. My gun is gone. Shit, I must've put it under my pillow already.

The knock sounds, more insistent this time. I can't pretend I'm not home. He knows. They all know. They're always watching.

More knocking, louder and louder.

"Leave me alone!" I scream and grab the nearest thing—the empty bottle—and hurl it at the door.

It shatters on impact, wine-coated glass raining down onto the wood floor.

"Evie?" His voice is muffled, but I'd know it anywhere.

"Lucius." I stand and wobble to the door. The glass is everywhere. My fuzzy slippers manage it fine until I step on a particularly large piece. "Fuck, ouch!"

"Evie, open the door."

"For you? No way!" I pick my foot up and try to look at the bottom, but I almost lose my balance.

"I'm not here to hurt you."

"Says the man who hurts me every chance he gets." I snort a laugh.

"You're drunk."

"What?"

"You're slurring your words."

I could swear I hear him mutter "lightweight."

"Go away."

"Who did you think it was? The man who put his hands on you?" The edge in his voice is sharper than the glass beneath my feet.

"Just leave."

"Let me in."

"No."

"Evie, I'm asking nicely."

"This is your 'nicely'?" I laugh, and I can admit it sounds a bit more hysterical than it should.

"Yes, but as you know, when I'm done asking, I'll turn to other methods."

I rest my forehead against the cool wood of the door. "Are you threatening me?"

"I'll break down this door, Evie. If you want to take that as a threat, go ahead."

The thing is, I believe him. I know Lucius will do whatever he wants, whenever he wants. That's part of the bad-boy appeal that had me swooning over him when I was young and dumb. A lifetime ago. Before I realized what he really is.

"I hate to do this, but then again, no I don't." His voice fades a little, and I imagine him backing away from the door and squaring up.

"You love violence. I know." I flip the deadbolts, moving slowly and missing one. Once I get them all, I pull open the door, the bottom scraping the glass along with it as it swings.

He looks me up and down, then focuses on my foot. "You really are a lightweight."

"Why won't you just leave me alone?" I hate the pleading tone of my voice, the desperation that winds its way through my words.

"Not my style." His light blue eyes should belong to an angel or a beautiful woman, but instead god bestowed them on Lucius. Why? To tempt me, I suppose. That's how the story goes, anyway.

"What are you mumbling about god?" He steps inside, sweeps me into his arms, and crunches the glass beneath his shoes. The door swings shut with a thud as he carries me into the living room. "Where's your room?"

I glance toward it. "I'm not telling you."

"You don't have to." He carries me close to his chest. Like he knows me. Like I'm important to him. When he puts me down on the edge of my tub, then kneels and pulls my foot up for inspection, I can almost convince myself that he's a dark-haired lover, someone who's here to take care of me, ravish me, worship me, save me. But then he looks up, and I remember that his good looks hide the corruption underneath.

"I'm fine. Please leave."

"You're not." He looks around. "Do you have any first aid stuff?"

"No."

His brows draw together. "Nothing? Not even alcohol?"

"Under the sink." I jerk my chin toward the vanity.

"I suppose that'll have to do." He stands and walks over to it, rolling his sleeves up as he goes. "Is your foot the only part of you that's hurt?"

How to answer that question. I can't. Instead, I giggle, and I *know* I sound insane. But I can't stop. Not when I see Lucius coming toward me with alcohol. My savior, ready to doctor my wound and comfort me as I spiral down, down, down—so far down that I'll drown in those blue eyes of his.

"You are talking nonsense." He peers closely at the

sole of my foot, then says, "There's glass here. I'm going to pull it out on the count of three. One, two—"

I scream.

He pours alcohol on the cut and then presses a towel to it.

Tears roll down my cheeks. "Y-you said three."

"I did," he agrees.

The alcohol burns and sends pain radiating up my leg. Lucius keeps the towel pressed tightly to the cut, his other hand gripping my calf.

I realize my robe is falling open. He does too, because his gaze climbs up my calf, my thigh, and then settles on my panties. It lights me on fire. It shouldn't. But shoulds and shouldn'ts don't matter anymore, not when my greatest enemy is in my home, doctoring my wounds, and making me feel things I'll regret.

"Regrets are pointless." He shakes his head.

Why do I keep saying things out loud? Jesus, get your shit together, Evie.

He pulls the towel away a little. "It's clotting. A relatively clean cut. You can avoid stitches as long as you don't do any tap-dancing anytime soon." Reaching to his neck, he loosens his tie and pulls it free. He places it on my foot, then starts wrapping it around, the deep purple fleur-de-lis pattern like a jewel against my skin.

"That looks expensive."

"It is." He tightens it and ties it off. When he's done, he inspects his work. "Teddy would be proud."

"The only good Vinemont. But still bad, of course." I wipe at my bleary eyes. "You're all bad."

"Fair enough." He stands and lifts me again with irritating ease. "You need to sleep it off."

"You're not sleeping here."

"Who said I was?" His goddamn smirk makes an appearance as he lays me on my bed. "Is this—" He pulls my gun from beneath my pillow and checks the chamber. "You keep a loaded gun under your pillow?"

I shrug.

He shrugs, too. "I'm not judging. Just don't accidentally shoot yourself." He replaces it, then pulls my blanket over me.

"I can't sleep with you here."

"Okay." He turns and walks out of my room.

Even in my drunken haze, I sit up and try to see where he's gone. Did he leave like I said? Ah, shit, the bastard is back, and now he's carrying a water.

"Drink." He sits beside me and presses the bottle into my hands. "You'll thank me in the morning."

"I'll never thank you."

"Okay."

"Stop saying 'okay.'"

"Okay."

Maddening, infuriating, asshole. He stares until I take the water and start drinking.

"Good girl."

Shit. Shit, shit, shit. I was not prepared for what

those words from his lips would do to me. I drink more and look anywhere but at him.

He leaves again, and I'm too fucking tired to care if he's raiding my pantry or stealing my leftovers, so I lie back down. After a short while, I hear him cleaning up the glass.

This is how I know I'm fucking drunk off my ass. In this weird drunk reality, Lucius Vinemont is in my apartment. He's not trying to kill me. In fact, he's doctoring my foot, making sure I hydrate, and cleaning up my mess. Yep, in real life, I'm probably passed out on the bathroom floor in a pool of my own vomit.

"Go back to sleep."

"Whoa, where'd you come from?" I look up to find him leaning on my bedroom door frame.

"Been here for two hours now, Evie. You've been snoring for the past hour of it. Then you stopped. What woke you? A dream?"

What? "I don't snore."

"Okay."

"Shut up." I turn my head to the side and close my eyes.

～

"EVIE." Lucius's voice. That mix of silken and deadly and deep.

"What?" I keep my eyes shut tight as my head starts to pound.

"Sun's up. Your hangover cocktail is beside you. Try not to get into any more trouble, would you darlin'? And lockup when I leave." Footsteps recede, and then I hear my front door close.

I crack my eyes open and quickly shut them again. Did … Did Lucius spend the night in my apartment? Holy shit. I press my palms to my forehead and groan as I remember bits and pieces of last night. I made mistake after mistake, the biggest one being that I let Lucius in. What was I thinking?

My foot aches dully, but my head is worse. I take a peek at my nightstand and find a neat line of pills and a glass with some sort of concoction in it. Trusting it seems unwise of me. Then again, Lucius was here all night and didn't so much as touch me after I got into bed.

In fact … I slept better than I have in a long time. But that must've just been the booze. Had to be. Like Lucius said, I'm a lightweight.

I roll over and grab the pills, pop them into my mouth, then drink them down. When I lie back, the room swims for a second, then settles down. It takes a while, but my thoughts finally start to coalesce into some semblance of sense. And then it hits me all over again—the party is tonight.

Screaming and crying aren't going to stop it from happening. Nothing will. I sit up and breathe through a few pounding aches in my skull that fade slowly.

I still can't believe Lucius was here all night. What

did he do? Sleep? I stand up, his tie still wrapped tightly around my injured foot, and walk into the living room. The couch doesn't look particularly rumpled. No, he didn't sleep.

Turning back around, I walk into my bedroom and stop. My heart does a stutter step, and I blink hard to make sure I'm seeing clearly. I am. I rush to my dresser and pull open the top drawer.

The black envelope is there, in the same place I'd left it. But I know. I *know* he searched through my things and found it. Maybe that's the reason he came here all along. He just got lucky that I was drunk enough to let him in without a fight. God, I'm making the same mistakes. That foolish little girl inside me is still pushing me in the wrong direction.

I back away and sit on my bed as the early rays of sunlight fight their way through my blinds.

My gaze travels back to my dresser, to that infernal invitation written in perfect calligraphy. He's seen the black paper, read it all.

He knows. He *knows* and left me alive. The silly little girl tries to tell me that Lucius doesn't want to harm me. That Lucius must know that I want no part of the Acquisition.

Maybe that's true, but I still can't trust him. And now, on top of everything, I have to wonder what Lucius is going to do with that information.

Knowing him, this party will turn into a massacre, a bloodletting at the very least. Even with that knowledge, I can't back out. Not if I want to live. I could warn them, let them know that the event is compromised. But that would lead to more questions, and eventually to Lucius. I have zero doubts they'd snuff me out with prejudice if they even suspected I'd somehow leaked it to a Vinemont. And on top of that ... I don't *want* to alert them. They are evil people who will stop at nothing to enforce their will on the world. I'll never help them. Not willingly.

No, I have to let this whole vicious scene play out.

My hands are tied. That sensation I felt yesterday, the hopelessness, comes back with a vengeance. But I can't drink another bottle of wine. Today, I need to be sharp. Because tonight is life or death.

My only question is, will Lucius see me as one of them?

19

LUCIUS

Little Teddy is already running around the front lawn when I pull up to the house. He stops tossing his football in the air and catching it when I get out of my car.

"Hey." He comes over and hugs my leg. "Whatcha doing?"

"Just need to talk to your dad."

"It's early." He backs away and tosses the football at me. It's a lame duck throw, but I manage to catch it anyway and flip it back to him.

It sails past him. "Sorry, little man."

"That's okay." He walks back to me. "Is this family business?"

I arch a brow. "Maybe."

"Can I come?"

"To what?"

"To whatever sort of business we got."

"You ready?" The front door swings open and Stella steps out. She's got a crossbow on one arm and a rifle hanging on her other shoulder.

"Yeah!" Teddy runs over to her, family business apparently forgotten.

"Lucius." Stella gives me a questioning look. "Everything all right?"

"All good." I give her a salute.

She doesn't look the least bit convinced. "I'll find out when I get back, I guess. Come on, Teddy. Let's go murder some bullseyes."

"I'm going to hit all of them!" He follows her to the ATV waiting outside the garage.

I trudge up to the porch and inside. "Sin?"

"In the office," he calls.

I meet him there and sink down on the leather couch.

"There's no way this is good news. You showing up here on a Saturday morning. I'm guessing this is something you didn't want to discuss over the phone." He pushes back from the desk and laces his fingers over his stomach. "What's happened?"

"Right on all points." I kick my feet up on the desk. He frowns.

"I spent the night with Evie."

He closes his eyes. "Didn't we *just* have a conversation about—"

"I didn't fuck her ... Yet."

"You spent the night with her, but you didn't fuck

her? I'm going to need an explanation, though I can assure you I don't *want* one."

"I was doing recon because Tyrone had to follow another lead. Speaking of—" I pull out my phone to check for messages from him. Nothing. He's been quiet since I sent him after the other tail. "Okay, yes, this is more bad news. Tyrone—I'm just spit balling here—is probably dead."

"What?"

"He found out someone else was tailing Evie, so I told him to stick to them and let me handle her. When the guy took off, he followed. I've messaged him a few times, but I haven't heard from him since."

"He's always reliable. Doesn't bode well."

I nod. "We should pour one out for him, I suppose."

"Lucius, it's nine in the morning."

"You're right. We should wait for at least ten. Anyway, I already know who we're dealing with."

"Beau Corrigan. You told me."

"Yes. But there's more." I pull out my phone and hand it to him.

"This is a photo of Evie sleeping," he says in an irritated monotone.

"Swipe left. Jeez."

His eyes pop open a little wider as he reads the invitation I found in her dresser. She'd tucked it in there gently, like it's a bomb that might explode at any minute. I suppose she had the right idea.

Sin moves the phone closer to his face. "Shit. That's tonight."

"Indeed it is. I'm going to swing by my place and pick up a tux, then head back to the city. I need to look dapper for this new foray into the Acquisition."

He stays silent for a while, rereading the invitation. "It's real." He tosses my phone down and leans back, letting his head loll on his shoulders. "They're really back. Fuck. We burned it to the ground, but here it is again. Like a goddamn weed."

I can hear the fatigue in him, the worry. After all, he almost lost Stella to this fucked up cabal.

"I should've rooted them out when they came for Teddy. But I guess ..." He sighs heavily. "I guess I was hoping that Leonard was acting alone. I should've known. I think I *did* know, but I couldn't face it, not after what Stella went through. I'll never let them touch her again." His voice hardens. "They'll never touch a hair on her head or the kids'. Not while I draw breath."

"We have to stop this now. If we don't, it could snowball. And if that happens—"

"They'll annihilate us all on principle. Turnabout is fair play, I suppose." He turns toward the sound of Renee and Rebecca giggling in the back den. "But I've never played fair, and I won't start now. I have too much to lose."

"Neither will I. I have a plan."

He meets my gaze again, and I swear he's aged a

few years since I first walked in. "Tell me, and do you have any cigarettes on you?"

"You know I quit."

He stares.

I get up. "Come on. I stashed a pack at the top of the pantry. Sort of an 'in case of emergency' thing."

"In that case, now's the time."

We get the cigs and walk out to the back porch. I pull off the wrapper and flick the lighter open. Just like riding a bike.

The first drag fills my lungs, and I remember why I loved smoking so much. The perfect burn. I pass it to Sin.

He takes a puff, then turns to me. "Tell me the plan. I'll tell you if it's shit."

"My plans are never shit."

A rifle cracks in the distance, and we settle in to hash it out. The two of us planning blood, murder, and sweet revenge—just like old times.

20

EVIE

Keeping a steady hand is difficult when I feel I want to vomit or simply collapse to the floor and fold into the fetal position. But I draw my eyeliner on straight, making a wing on the corner and filling it in.

Simple strokes.

Step by step.

That's the way I'm going to make it through tonight.

I don't know what comes after, but I have no illusions about these people. I'm walking into a den of vipers. I could die there. That thought doesn't hit me as hard as it should. Maybe because I'm more afraid of the alternative—joining them. I won't do it, but I already know there are no choices for me in any of this. The Acquisition doesn't bargain. It demands. Either you give in to those demands, or you're crushed under the weight of hundreds of years of violence and malice.

Once my eyes are done, I finish the foundation and add little touches of sheen to my cheeks. Satisfied, I walk to my closet and pluck out the dress. It's beautiful. Lace that clings and flows in all the right places. Looking the part they want me to play.

If I can fake it, then maybe I'll survive and stay out of the Acquisition. That's what I hope for, despite knowing they'll never let me go.

For the millionth time, I regret coming back here. Taking Lucius down should've been simple—well, as simple as corporate sabotage can be. It's been anything but.

I check myself in the mirror and add earrings and a simple sapphire necklace.

My foot aches, but I slide it into a red-bottomed heel. I still have Lucius's tie. My blood is on it. I should've tossed it into the trash when I took it off the wound, but I didn't. Instead, I'd stared at it for far too long, as if I could read my future there in the swirling fleur-de-lis stained crimson.

I take a deep breath and put on my mask. Not the one in the gilded box by the door, the one I'll have to wear for the rest of the night, no matter what. Haughty and condescending—it's the language of these people. They've grown accustomed to ruling and abusing anyone they consider beneath them, so the trick is to make sure they believe I'm at their level, or preferably, higher.

My mother told me about this arena, about what would happen when I married one of the Southern elite. *"You never know, Evie dear, your husband may be in the running for Sovereign one day."* My mother's voice echoes through me. She was a cold woman, one who eagerly took part in the Acquisition trials. She was so proud of Red when he was chosen to compete.

For some reason, I don't idealize my parents, don't even mourn them. They're dead because of Lucius and his family, yet I feel ... nothing. Nothing at all for them. I suppose it's because they never tried to save me from the Acquisition penalty, never warned me my life was on the line. They played along willingly, despite what it meant for me.

I can't dwell on them—other than adopting my mother's icy mannerisms. I push my shoulders back and grab my black mask, then head down to the lobby. The elevator stops early, opening on the fifth floor.

When the elevator door opens, I back up. The man is wearing a black tux, his blond hair swept back in a neat style that reminds me of fascists and goose-steps. He must've planned this, catching me off guard on this floor so I'd go along with him.

"You look ..." The man lets his gaze fall down my body, then back to my eyes. "Lovely."

"I told you I don't need an escort." I straighten my spine and move to hit the button for the lobby again.

He grabs my arm in the same spot he'd bruised. "I didn't ask."

"I can't imagine the Sovereign would appreciate your manhandling of me."

"You think this is manhandling?" He licks his lips and glances at mine. "I'd like to show you what real manhandling feels like, Evie. Would you like that?"

"Considering I find you repulsive and haven't even bothered to get your name, I don't think I would."

His grip tightens. "That aristocratic mouth of yours is going to get you into trouble. You can call me Sir or Charles."

I give a bored sigh. "If we're done here, I have a party to get to."

"My car's out front." He finally steps back from me.

"How nice for you." I pull my fob from my bag. "I'll be driving myself."

"You know, the Sovereign warned me you'd be difficult, that you'd think you could somehow avoid your responsibilities and buck our claim to you." He leans closer. "But I told him I can handle you."

"That's a cute story. Excuse me." I try to move past him.

He doesn't let me go. "Oh, Evie."

The way he says my name makes my hackles rise. Then with a force that makes my teeth rattle, he slams my back against the wall by the elevator bank. It takes my breath away, and he cages my neck with his meaty palm.

"Now you're going to walk out of here on my arm and get into my waiting car. No more talking. No more bullshit, Evie. You will *not* embarrass me tonight."

"You're doing that fine all by yourself." I struggle to get the words out, but I do.

His nostrils flare, and his grip tightens. "You stupid bitch."

The doorway to the stairs opens. "Oh, pardon me, I didn't realize the room was taken."

I make a small noise that gets caught in my constricted throat, because I know that voice. I know it so well that I hear it when I'm alone, when I'm asleep, when I'm daydreaming.

The man releases me the moment Lucius's fist collides with his face.

I gasp for breath as Charles goes down, his body hitting the tile floor with a hard thump. He's large, like a roided-out prize fighter. But Lucius is fast.

Lucius jumps on top of him, his fists flying. The sounds of impact make my stomach churn, but Lucius doesn't stop. He's on fire, his animal rage and power on full display.

Though it takes a massive effort, Charles finally throws him off, then both men get to their feet. They circle each other, fists up, as I back away.

"Vinemont trash." Charles spits a wad of blood onto the floor.

Someone opens their apartment door just down

the hall, then quickly slams and locks it when they get a look at what's happening.

"At least I don't go around telling people to call me sir." Lucius sneers. "Douche move."

Charles lunges forward, but his fist misses Lucius, and he swings wildly. Lucius lands a vicious punch to his lower back, and Charles staggers past me. I stick my foot out, and when he trips and starts to fall, Lucius shoots me a grin.

"Nice." He follows Charles to the ground again, turns him over, and lands blow after blow on his face. "This is for the bruises. For touching her. For hurting her. For thinking you could control her." He punctuates each statement with pure violence.

Split-lipped and bloody-nosed, Charles bucks him again, and Lucius rolls away, then jumps to his feet with feline quickness.

"I own her." Charles points at me and spits more blood. "If you try to take her from me, I'll make sure you suffer."

"Are you threatening me?" Lucius shakes his head, his fists still up. "Maybe you should've tried that *before* I kicked your ass. At this point, it just sounds kind of hollow, you know?"

I've backed into the elevator doors, tucking myself against them. I left my pistol at home, even though I didn't want to, because there's no way I would've been allowed into the party with a weapon. Now I'm wishing I'd tried it anyway.

"It's not a threat, Vinemont. It's a fact. Evie is my property."

"Fuck you!" I yell it before I even know what I'm doing.

Lucius grins. "I don't think she agrees with your claim, *sir*." He glances my way. "Is this the one who bruised you?" His tone turns feral at the end, as if he already knows the answer and doesn't like it one bit.

I nod.

"It doesn't matter. She's mine, and once I've killed you, I'll go to work on the rest of your family."

"Excellent game plan," Lucius taunts. "Too bad you're failing so miserably at step one."

Charles jabs. Lucius ducks, then slams his fist into Charles's midsection.

The brute lets out an *oof* noise and stumbles back again.

"This is fun. Don't get me wrong." Lucius reaches inside his coat—only now do I realize he's wearing a tux—and pulls out a blade. "But I have somewhere to be, and I hate to keep my stunning date waiting." He throws me a glance.

Charles runs at him, tackling him to the ground. I yell with surprise at the sudden onslaught. Charles grips Lucius's wrist and slams it against the floor again and again until he drops the knife, which skitters across the tile toward me.

Charles wraps his hands around Lucius's throat. "When I'm through with your family, nothing will be left. I will burn them alive, the same way you did to my family. And I'll piss on the ashes."

Lucius fights, punching and struggling against Charles. I look down. The blade is between us. My vision tunnels, and I stare at the glinting blade. Can I do this? I already killed a man once. Surely, I can do it again. Especially to Charles. Especially when Lucius is in trouble.

I drop the bag I've been clutching and snatch up the blade. Charles doesn't look at me, doesn't even know I've come up behind him.

My hands shake, but I won't let this bastard kill Lucius. If anyone gets to do that, it's me. I bring the blade up and prepare to slam it down into his back, but then Charles groans and falls sideways off Lucius.

Lucius sits up and cracks his neck, then gets to his feet as Charles crawls away, leaving a bloody trail on the pale floor.

"Darlin'." He takes the blade from my hand. "We should be going. We wouldn't want to be late." His tone is so easy, not at all indicative of the fact he's been fighting for his life.

Charles turns over and flops onto his back, a knife embedded in his stomach. He yells, the sound rattling down the long hallway.

"I'll finish this for you, and then we'll go. Sound good?" He kisses the back of my hand. "Good." He turns back to Charles as the man pulls himself to his feet.

Flipping the blade in the air, Lucius catches it with ease and advances on Charles. "I love a good gutting. Really gets the blood up."

Is this man—the one I tried to kill, the one who took my brother from me, the one I've vowed to ruin—is he going to kill for me? I think I might be going crazy. Or maybe the rollercoaster of the past week is making me force connections where there aren't any. After all, Lucius is a killer. Killing Charles is well within his nature. But he said it was for me. For *me*.

Lucius goes for him, his body taut and controlled, like a lethal cat stalking prey.

Charles, one hand around the blade in his gut, dodges to the left, ramming through the door into the stairwell. Lucius follows him through the door, and then I hear a fading scream and a sick thud.

Lucius yanks open the stairway door again. "Shit. He launched himself off the rail. He's a few stories down."

Another apartment door opens, and a woman in a robe with a towel around her hair hurries out. "Did you hear that scream? I was in the shower and ..."

Lucius stows his knife before the woman notices.

"What's happened?" She narrows her eyes at him and then focuses on the blood marring the floor. "What's that? It leads to the stairwell."

"We have to go." Lucius takes my elbow and leads me to the elevator. Two more doors open—the residents probably emboldened by the shower woman.

The doors open, and we step onto the elevator as if this is a completely normal evening. We're just a couple on a date, not two people who fought off an attacker who then fell to a grisly end.

I'm practically stupefied, my thoughts congealing as he leads me through the lobby and out the front door. He stops before we reach a black sedan on the curb. When he puts his hands up to cup my face, something inside me that's been on a knife's edge seems to back off. I can breathe. I can look into his eyes and calm myself.

"It's a good bet the fall killed him. Especially since his guts were already falling into his hands. But if not, I'm going to kill him for you, Evie. I swear it. I won't let him hurt you." He presses his forehead to mine. "Do you believe me?"

"Yes." I say it without hesitation.

"Good." He pulls back, his gaze darting to my lips for only a split second. Then he opens the back of the car and helps me in.

We take off as sirens wail nearby.

"If you walk into the Sovereign's party, you'll never walk back out again." My voice shakes as I peer at him in the dark back seat of the car.

"An excellent point. Noted and discarded." He moves closer. "Come here. You're shivering."

I don't fight as Lucius wraps his arm around me. I don't protest when he kisses my forehead and smooths my hair back into place. That soothing sensation is there in each of his touches, in every brush of his fingertips against my skin. It's wrong that he makes me feel this way, but I can't deny it. And right now?

Right now, I *need* it.

Right now, I need Lucius.

21

LUCIUS

*E*vie takes her small black bag when I offer it.
"Thank you. I didn't even think to grab it." She opens it and pulls out a compact, flips it open, and peers at herself in the mirror.

"I wanted to tell you how beautiful you look in that dress."

She falters for a second, then goes back to wiping beneath her eyes and freshening her lipstick. "Thank you."

"How long have you known about the party invitation?"

She returns the compact to her bag and closes it perfunctorily. "Why did you go through my things?"

"Why wouldn't I?"

She turns to me. "Why were you there tonight? What do you think crashing an Acquisition party is going to accomplish?"

"I'm going to take names, darling. I need to know my enemy. Once I have them all, I'll do a little more research for the stragglers, and then I'll hunt them all down."

"You didn't answer my first question." She leans into me slightly as the driver takes a turn at quick clip. Her perfume is light, floral. Perfect for her.

"I was there to pick you up."

We're so close here in the car, and I want to claim her mouth, to kiss down her throat and undress her slowly, savoring each bit of skin as it's revealed to me. I've never wanted to go slow with anyone, never wanted to take my time to discover each curve and ridge, each sigh and moan.

"Why are you looking at me like that?" she asks with a breathy voice.

"I can't look at you?"

She swallows. "Not like that, no."

I lean closer, and she doesn't move away. "I think you know I've always been a fan of breaking the rules."

When her gaze flutters to my mouth, I take a chance and nuzzle her neck, grazing my lips along her soft skin.

"I can't do this."

"That's okay. I can." I open my mouth and suck her skin between my lips, tasting her.

"Lucius."

Fuck, the way she says my name lights a fire in my

blood. I kiss lower, grazing the edge of her dress, and then I pull back.

Her pupils are blown, her lips parted.

I kiss her. Not gently, not a request. I take this kiss. One hand at the back of her neck, the other at her waist. When her tongue dances against mine, my restraint—what little I had—evaporates. I press her against the seat, claiming and sucking and licking. She grips my jacket, her body pushing back against me, giving me every bit of friction and touch. I can't stop kissing her. Angling her head so I can go deeper, feel more, take more. She's giving me life, and I will happily take life if it means I get to experience this again.

She bites my lip. I taste blood and give it back to her, kissing and overcoming her, making her feel how small she is against me, how easily I can give her pleasure and pain. Fuck, I want to take her right here, right now. To lift up that dress and make her straddle me, take me all the way inside.

"Lucius." She pants against my mouth, her heart frantic against my own. Chest to chest, face to face, we take each other's measure.

"I want you, Evie. And not just quick and dirty right now. I want more."

She takes a shuddering breath. "No."

"No doesn't mean anything to me when it comes to you." I kiss her again, harsh and claiming.

She responds, her tongue lashing against mine as

the car finally slows to a stop. I run my hand up her waist and cup her breast through the lace. Her nipple is taut and wanting. It needs my tongue, my teeth.

"Please, we can't." She presses her palms to my cheeks, her skin burning just like mine. "We have to survive tonight. We have to. And then ... Then we can figure this out."

"I don't need to figure anything out." I kiss her once more, a final touch in the dark back seat. "I know what I want."

She gulps a breath as I back off.

"We're going to finish this, Evie. You can lie to yourself all you want, but you and me—we're going to happen. We've been on this path for years, we just didn't know it." A collision course, more aptly, I suppose.

"You shouldn't do this. You can't go in there and expect them not to realize who you are. They'll know." She pulls out her compact again.

I wipe at the lipstick I'm certain is smeared on my mouth. "They aren't as smart as you seem to think they are."

"It's not a matter of smart. They have eyes and ears everywhere. When Charles doesn't show up, they'll be on high alert."

"You know so much about them?" I ask.

She reapplies her lipstick. "I grew up with it. So did you."

"Fair point." Pulling back, I turn and look out the

window at the large Mediterranean estate. Palm trees line the entrance, and beyond them a fountain pisses water into the sky. I'm a ridiculously wealthy man, but I still find this sort of excess pathetic. It's all a show, one intended to impress other rich assholes. Well, from one rich asshole to another, I'm not fucking impressed.

"Shit." I flex my aching fists.

"What is it?"

"I forgot to get a shot in for Tyrone."

"Who?"

"Just an associate of mine I suspect that Hitler Youth motherfucker killed." He got in some decent face shots on me, and I can tell the left side of my face is a touch swollen.

I reach into the back window and pull out my mask.

"Plague doctor?" She frowns at it. "You don't think that's a bit much?" She pulls hers from her bag. It's a lacy black mask with sapphires along the top edge.

"I think it'll be a hit." I reach for the door handle, but pause and ask, "Are you ready?"

She laughs, but it's tight and dark. "Ready to go to a party with people who might want to kill me, with a man they definitely want to kill, and with no idea what sort of terrors await? Sure. Why not?"

"That's the spirit, darlin'." I open the car door and stand, then help her out.

She's unsteady on her injured foot at first, but she

keeps a hold on my arm as we walk up the front steps and past two armed sentries by the fountain.

At the front door, there's an arbor full of sweetly-scented jasmine overhead, along with a man ushering guests. Three people enter ahead of us, and then we're greeted by the man in the lime green half-face mask.

"Welcome. Unfortunately, after some recent events, the Sovereign isn't allowing weapons into this particular evening's revelries. Are either of you armed?"

"I beg your pardon." The tone in Evie's voice crackles like a cattle prod. "Do you think I could conceal a weapon in this dress? Or are you threatening to search me like I'm some sort of common criminal? Is that it?"

The lime green dodo stammers a few times, then closes his mouth before trying again. "Of course not. My apologies, Miss ..." He pulls out an iPad and opens a document.

"Evie Witherington." She says it with cold confidence, as if she owns this place and everyone in it.

If my cock wasn't already hard for her, it certainly would be now.

"The guest of honor, top of the list. Welcome, mademoiselle. And your escort?" He peers at me as he makes a note in his document.

Without missing a beat, she scoffs. "Don't you know Charles? Honestly. The Sovereign should hire better help."

The man snaps his gaze back to her, and I don't even try to hide my grin.

"Yes, yes of course. My apologies. Please, right this way." He turns and leads us past the open courtyard with yet another fountain and into the main house.

"Quite impressive," I whisper in her ear. "You're practically a dominatrix, aren't you? I think you made him cream his pants."

"Focus," she hisses.

Classical music plays softly somewhere farther in, and people chat with each other in various spots throughout the ornate foyer. The crowd is large yet sparser than I remember. The new Sovereign doesn't have anywhere near the adherents as in years past. I like to think my family has everything to do with the thinning numbers.

"—haven't seen him in weeks. His wife is worried." A conversation floats across the marble-tiled room. "Leonard doesn't do things like this. And he certainly wouldn't have missed this event."

I smile. They'll only find Leonard if they don scuba gear and have hands-on experience in gutting swamp gators.

"Beau said not to worry about it. So I think we should be more careful, but Leonard will probably turn up and …" The conversation fades as we enter the main ballroom. More people mingle in here, some of them along the shadowy corners or bunched up in alcoves along the wall.

Pressing my lips to Evie's ear, I whisper. "This is where we part ways. For now."

She lets go of my arm, then grabs it again. "Be careful."

"Worried about me?" I run my fingers along her wrist.

"Worried someone will kill you before I get the chance." She pulls her hand away, but not before I catch her glancing at my lips again.

I slip back and move into a group of people having a conversation about the latest short sell fiasco in the markets. But I keep my eye on Evie, on the woman who catches everyone's eye the moment she passes.

The crowd here seems to be a curious combination of the rather old and the quite young. Makes sense, I suppose, given that the ones in the prime of their lives five years ago are all dust now.

"Is that Evie Witherington?" Someone to my right asks.

An older woman in a jewel-crusted mask says, "I don't know, but she looks about the right age."

"She looks ripe." An old man in a beaded mask leers.

I could break his neck and disappear, but that's not what I'm here for. He'll just have to wait his turn.

A man breaks away from the largest group at the back of the ballroom near the small string quartet. He wears a midnight blue mask with white feathers at the temples. Something in his bearing tells me exactly who he is. Beau Corrigan.

I edge closer to where Evie stands alone, her mouthwatering figure set off perfectly in her dress and heels. She's a feast for the eyes, and plenty of the sick motherfuckers in this room are ready and waiting at the buffet line.

The room gets quieter, everyone watching the Sovereign approach her.

"Evie Witherington." He smiles big. "I'm so pleased you could make it." He takes her hand in his.

"Thank you for the invitation." She dips her chin only a little. Good girl.

"My pleasure. When I heard you were back in town, I knew we had to do something big to welcome you back to your family." He smiles at her. "This is, after all, where you belong."

"Thank you."

He still hasn't released her hand. It's making me fucking itchy.

"We're a bit smaller than before, but we still like a good party. Might I have a dance with you, Evie?"

She glances around, and I know she's searching for me in the crowd. But I've already blended in. Like she said, I was raised in this. I know exactly how to play my part.

"Of course." She smiles. It's strained and wrong, but he doesn't know that.

So he leads her deeper into the room and motions

to the quartet to play something I'm certain he already pre-selected for just this moment. These fools are always so predictable. In both their boring moments as well as their violent sprees.

I want to keep an eye on her, but I also need to get my hands on the iPad I saw earlier. The guest list—that's money. The plan I sold to Sin was for me to break into the Sovereign's office while I'm here, do some real James Bond shit, and leave with the names. But now that I know it's all conveniently typed into that smarmy greeter's iPad, all I have to do is swipe it. Once that's done, I can take Evie and get the fuck out of here.

Easy peasy.

22

EVIE

The Sovereign pulls me tightly against him as we start a stiff waltz. It's been a long time since I took dance classes, but it seems those lessons were beaten into me enough by my dance teacher that I remember the steps with mechanical ease.

"I was worried you'd decide against coming to greet your family at this little get-together." He knows the steps by heart, too, and he leads me with careful attention to the people gathered around. They watch us through their masks, only shadowy holes where their eyes should be.

"I wouldn't miss it."

"Is that so?" He spins me with the cadence of the music, but I don't feel like this is a dance at all. It's more of a hostage negotiation. Only, I'm the one who's the hostage.

"My family has always taken part in the Acquisition."

"That's correct. In fact, I'd venture to say you're one of the bedrock families of this institution. That's why it was so wonderful when you returned to your home. The Witherington roots are still strong, and I want you to know that I personally want to ensure that those roots grow even deeper."

"That's very kind of you."

His piercing eyes seem to bore into me as we continue our dance. He's younger than I expected. Perhaps mid-forties or so. Sovereigns don't have any specific age requirement. The only true requirement is cruelty, as far as I recall. Then again, it's not as if he went through the trials and came out victorious. He was chosen by default since there hasn't been a Sovereign for five years nor any mechanism through which to choose one.

"You were elected?" I ask to break up his unflinching stare.

"It wasn't a true democratic process, but yes, I earned the trust of several of our older members. The last coronation event was such a blow to the organization that we needed leadership as soon as possible, and it simply couldn't wait. But, I can assure you I know the rules, and I will step down from my duties as Sovereign after the next Acquisition trials take place and a winner is declared."

My lungs seem to constrict at his words. "You're running the trials?"

"Absolutely." He smiles. "We must honor the old ways, don't you think?"

I nod while inside I'm screaming.

"I'm glad we're of the same mind, which brings me to another topic of concern."

Here it goes. Whatever vicious purpose he has in his grand plan, this is where it will come out.

"What is that?" I ask as he spins me in a wider arc across the floor.

"There has been talk." He purses his lips, then continues, "Not that I put much stock in talk, you see. But, even so, there has been talk that Lucius Vinemont has been skulking around you. Have you met with him?"

"I have to meet with him." I smile tightly. "I'm going to gut his company and leave it in ruins."

He returns my smile, and his is actually genuine. "That's what I needed to hear. Thank you, Evie."

I'm starting to get a little dizzy. Not from the dance, but more from the pressure on my injured foot. It aches with each step I take.

"Now that we have that behind us, let's move on to the more pleasant aspect of our relationship."

I absolutely do *not* like the sound of that. So, naturally, I smile. "What did you have in mind?"

"The topic might seem a bit delicate, and I apologize if this is forward of me, but because we are in the rebuilding stage, we need to increase our numbers."

"You'd like me to recruit?" I say it with as much snobbery as I can muster.

He laughs. "Oh, certainly nothing so vulgar as that. No, no. You see, my nephew Charles has taken quite a shine to you." He glances at the crowd. "He's here somewhere, probably watching your every move like everyone else. You truly are breathtaking, my dear."

"Thank you." My heart, already beating at a rabbit's pace, kicks up another fearful notch. But I keep my face neutral, my tone cool. I have to. If I give even a hint about what's going on inside me right now, I won't leave this house alive.

"No need to thank me. It's the truth. Now, Charles is young like you, and he is hungry. He wants to be Sovereign so badly, and I have zero doubts he would win the Acquisition with ease. More importantly, he will make an excellent husband, and he is fully capable of fathering many, many children with a pure, true bloodline. The two of you could do so much for this family, wouldn't you agree?"

I don't know if it's the pain in my foot, the horrible future Beau Corrigan just painted for me, or the fact that I'm hovering on the edge of terror—but I start to feel faint.

"Are you all right?" He slows his feverish pace. "You've gone pale beneath your mask, my dear."

"I'm fine. I think I might need some air."

"My apologies. Allow me to escort you outside." He offers me his arm.

I don't want to take it, but I don't know if I'll be able to make it outside without it. So, I do what I must and walk out into the muggy night with him. He motions to a passing server and grabs two flutes of champagne, clutching them between the fingers of one hand.

"I realize I may have rushed in where angels fear to tread." He sits me on the edge of yet another fountain and stands before me. "You have a lot to think about. I don't expect an answer for Charles right this second." He taps the watch on his wrist. "But time won't wait forever. It's best to get an early start on children, especially when there's so much on the line."

I can only look up at him and wonder what sort of mental disease would lead him to believe I'd ever touch Charles of my own free will.

"Here." He hands me a champagne flute. "Let's drink to a bright future."

I want to say no, but the insistent nature of this man tells me that's not an option. "To a bright future." I lift my glass and drink as he downs his.

"We really have a chance to make the Acquisition something even more lasting for future generations. Yes, we have some wrinkles. The Vinemonts being one of them."

I can second that statement, though I must say Lucius has been far more than just a wrinkle for me.

He's something much more insidious—someone I want to trust even though I know it's a bad idea.

"And don't let me dissuade you from doing your job on Magnolia. We all want to see that company go down in flames. But once that's done, it would be far better for you to turn your attention to being a wife, a mother, and a strong member of the society. Wouldn't you agree?"

"If you all hate the Vinemonts so much, why haven't you killed them?" I don't know why I ask it, but as soon as I do, I'm curious to hear the answer.

He seems taken aback by my question, the white feathers on the edges of his mask swaying a little. "An interesting query." He clasps his hands at his back and paces slowly in front of me. "To answer it, let me give a little back story that you already know quite well. At the final ceremony of the last Acquisition five years ago, a Sovereign was chosen."

"Sinclair Vinemont."

"Precisely." He turns on his heel and continues pacing. "But then—for reasons unknown to me—he decided to turn on his fellow friends and family and start a fire that burned down generations of good families."

I'm trying to follow, but I catch myself glancing around, hoping for a glimpse of Lucius. He shouldn't even be here, but now I wonder where he is. Surely he hasn't been caught?

"The laws of our society are clear. Concerning the

Sovereign, no one can make a move against the Sovereign during their ten-year term. The Sovereign is sacrosanct, untouchable, and his—or her—" He gives me a simpering smile. "—family is part of that untouchable unit. I suppose to prevent kidnapping and extortion attempts, but I digress." He waves a hand. "As the Acquisition does not have a mechanism for abdication, and the choice of Sovereign is absolute once made, the laws of our society still apply."

I can't believe what I'm hearing. "Are you saying Sinclair Vinemont is still the Sovereign?"

He stops in front of me. "I'm saying that we live and die by the rules written down by the first families to participate in the Acquisition. We can't follow them piecemeal. They are the underpinnings of everything we do here. I'm currently serving as *interim* Sovereign in the true Sovereign's absence. As I've said, we will have the trials in the near future as is required in our laws. Until then, I will continue steering the ship."

No words form themselves on my lips. Nothing. How could they still be following this legalistic nonsense when the Vinemonts are the very reason they have to rebuild at all? I'm not saying I want them all wiped off the face of the earth—admittedly, a fairly recent development in my mindset. But I'm also fairly certain that the original founders of the Acquisition would've had the Vinemonts hunted down and ripped apart.

"That's not to say we haven't had a few members try

to take matters into their own hands. But that's neither here nor there." He clasps his hands together. "Enough talk of the law. May I have another dance?"

I give him a coquettish smile. "I wouldn't want Charles to get jealous."

"Indeed." He gives me a slight bow. "Please return inside when you're ready. I'd like to present you to the assemblage."

"Of course." At this point, I'd rather chew glass.

"And Evie?"

"Yes?"

"I sincerely regret what happened to Red. He was a fierce competitor. I saw him at the third trial." He sighs like it's a fond memory. "The way he took control and proved to everyone that he had the stomach for being Sovereign. It really was a sight to behold."

"Thank you." I say it as graciously as I can despite the blood draining from my face. Despite *knowing* he's talking about how my brother killed a woman in cold blood. Hung her right in front of her own daughter to prove just how vicious and depraved he could be.

"See you inside." He returns to the party, his black tux like a smudge on the night.

I take a breath, then another. My gorge keeps rising, and I have to fight it down. I wasn't at the last Acquisition, mainly because I wasn't out in society yet. My mother had strict rules on where I could and couldn't be seen. With that said, I think she would've allowed me to accompany her to the trials if Red hadn't vehemently forbidden it. I remember being *hurt* that he commanded I stay home. I thought he didn't want me getting in the way of him winning the Acquisition. Because I knew in my heart that my big brother would win it all.

I was such a fool. More and more, I realize Red showed me one tiny sliver of his true self. The only bright part of him, the slimmest shard that could still love and protect someone. The rest of him ... Well, I know about that part now. About all the horrible things he did to win, but also to protect me. It's all so twisted up—love with duty, protection with pain. Red brutalized people. Some of it he did for me, but not all. It was never all for me.

The music turns livelier as the partiers take over the dance floor.

After waiting as long as seems safe, I rise and walk toward the French doors that open onto the veranda. My foot aches, and I still search through the crowd for Lucius.

Beau catches my eye and motions for me to join him at the front of the ballroom. I can't deny him, no matter how much I wish I could just back away and disappear.

I step into the ballroom, then yelp as someone grabs me from behind.

"There you are." Hot breath hits my neck, and I flinch as Charles yanks me against him, his hold on me as terrifying as it is unyielding.

23

LUCIUS

"No ... I just had it." The man with the lime green mask leans over and peers into the bushes by his greeting station as I tuck his iPad into my jacket.

This was easier than I thought. A little misdirection, and now I have the keys to this fucked-up kingdom.

Edging away, I skirt around the fountain as Lime Green, panic in his tone, calls to the sentries out front. "Did anyone come through here?"

I keep going into the foyer, a skip in my step. Now all I need to do is collect Evie and get the fuck out of this shark tank.

When I enter the ballroom, I see the Sovereign up front on a small stage. A gasp goes through the crowd—everyone looking at something up ahead and to the right.

A sinking feeling swirls in my gut, and I edge my way forward. I can't find Evie. Even in this dim room with everyone in masks, I would know her the moment I saw her. But she isn't here.

"Charles?" Beau Corrigan calls from his spot at the front of the room. "What are you—"

"She's with him! With Lucius Vinemont!"

The people in the room hiss, and some even cross themselves unironically. I push my way forward until I see her. That blond motherfucker has one arm around her waist, squeezing her against him as he walks her forward. He's surprisingly spry for a man who was holding his guts in his hand only hours ago.

"Charles, I believe you're mistaken. Come, let's talk about this." Beau steps from the stage and hurries through the crowd.

Charles is bruised and bloodied, a white bandage wrapped around his middle.

"Get your hands off me!" Evie stomps Charles's foot.

"Shit." He shakes her like a doll, but he doesn't let her go. "Shut your fucking mouth."

If I didn't already intend to kill this man, those words would've sealed it. No one speaks to her that way.

"Move." Beau steps in front of them. "Now, Charles, please release Evie. She's our guest."

"She's a fucking traitor. I saw her with Lucius. She *helped* him."

Beau frowns, his ridiculous feathery mask drooping a bit. "Is that true, Evie?"

"Of course it's true." She struggles against Charles's hold. "How do you think I'm going to take him down? I have to get close to him."

"Bullshit." Charles grabs her hair and pulls it.

She shrieks, and I tense to strike.

"Charles! I demand you release her this instant!" Beau bellows.

Charles glowers, but he puts her on her feet. She sways for a moment, then moves to stand by Beau. Smart.

"She's lying." Charles presses his hand to the bandage at his waist. "They're together. She helped him do this to me." He tilts his head up and scans the crowd. "He's here."

"Lucius?" Beau asks.

The fear in his tone is so satisfying, just like the whoosh of dismay rippling through the crowd. Some are already slipping out into the foyer, perhaps fearing a repeat of five years ago.

"Yes, Lucius is here." He turns toward the quartet. "Knock that shit off! Everyone, turn on the lights. Take off your masks!"

"Charles, please." Beau strides to him. "You're embarrassing me." He hisses.

Evie backs away. She's limping, her foot probably killing her right now.

"I'm saving your goddamn life." Charles glares at him.

I follow her trajectory as she tries to melt into the small crowd.

"Masks off now!" Charles yells as the lights overhead flicker to life.

Fuck. I cut through a group of people and get to Evie.

When I touch her, she somehow knows it's me, because she leans into me.

"We have to get out of here," she whispers, her eyes huge beneath the mask. "If they see you…"

"I know." I take her hand and pull her away from Charles, away from the people who are removing their masks.

We're almost to the foyer when the doors slam closed.

I skid to a stop and turn.

"Shit." I pull Evie behind me.

The entire room is staring at us. Maskless faces with hearts full of spite.

Charles stalks through the middle of them, parting them like a cursed red sea. "There. You see? She's whoring herself out to a fucking Vinemont."

I whip my mask off and toss it to the floor. The gasp that quakes through the room is once again, so, so gratifying. "I'm going to make you eat those words right along with this knife." I pull out my blade.

Charles brandishes the same knife I used to stab him. "You aren't leaving here with her."

"You aren't leaving here at all." I itch to destroy him, but I wait. He needs to move a little closer, deeper into the spider's web.

"How did you get in here?" Beau jogs up behind Charles, his eyes practically popping out of his pale face.

"Does it matter?" I smirk. "Just send your little fuckboy over here so I can put him out of his misery. I hate leaving a job unfinished." I point the tip of my knife at the blood blooming along his bandaged midsection.

The Sovereign straightens and pushes his shoulders back as he holds out a hand. "Evie, come away from him. Come to me. We're your family."

I hold her tighter, some small part of me fearing she'll accept his invitation.

"Family?" she asks. "Does family leave bruises?" She jerks her chin at Charles. "Does family threaten and intimidate and harass?"

Beau turns to Charles. "Have you hurt her?"

Charles glowers at us, his gaze never leaving Evie. "She's mine to hurt."

"I'm not yours, and I'll *never* be yours." The venom in her voice turns me on, but I have to remind my cock I'm currently in a life-or-death situation.

"Charles, what have you done?" Beau scolds.

"I've done what is my right to do," Charles barks. "You promised her to me."

"I did, but these things need finesse." Beau holds up his hands.

The rest of the guests have receded, backing away from the scene, but still watching as they whisper amongst themselves.

"Lovely family spat and all, but I think it's time we were going. Have to leave fashionably early, you know?" I back up until Evie is against the rear doors. I can hear her trying the handles to no avail.

"Evie, I'm sorry Charles has overstepped his place when it comes to you, but we can make this right." Beau, like an idiot, is still trying to win over a woman who wants no part of this fucking farce.

"So I can be your broodmare?" She bangs on the doors. "No, thanks!"

"You're going to be my wife, the mother of my children."

"Charles, stand down!" Beau yells.

That's when I see the crazy click into place—the same crazy he had in his eyes at Evie's place. He's so off kilter I'm beginning to suspect he's got dueling banjos in his family tree.

"You can't take her away from me. She's mine." Charles grips the hilt tighter.

"She isn't yours until I say so. I'm the interim Sovereign!" Beau sputters, his face turning red. "The laws of this—"

"Enough of this bullshit! Fuck your stupid rules, and fuck you!" Charles whirls on Beau and slices out with my blade.

Beau reaches for his neck as Charles turns back to me and charges.

I shove Evie to the side and dodge his blade. It embeds in the wood doors at my back, and Charles tries to yank it free.

Screams erupt all around as people start running.

"Lucius!" Evie pulls me back, following the flow of the crowd.

Beau falls to his knees, his hands at his throat as blood gushes between his fingers. He's a goner.

Charles is a straight-up psycho. Damn.

"Come on!" Evie screams.

I give Charles one more look as he wrenches the blade free from the door. He charges me again, but a woman gets in his way, and he slices her face open with a wild swing. Her scream cuts through the din, then fades behind me.

Evie's still limping, but she's hurrying through the room and toward the doors that lead to an outer courtyard. The guests are all running for the same exit.

"Go!" I push her into the mass of bodies, then turn right as Charles plunges his knife straight into my chest.

Evie's scream is loud in my ears as I fall back and get carried in the stampede for the courtyard doors.

Charles shoves people out of his way to get to me,

but I gain my feet right when I reach the doors. Evie is there waiting for me, her face wan and pale as I wrench the knife from my chest, then scoop her into my arms.

I run. I run like I'm a fucking Olympic star looking to three-peat. Evie clings to me, her arms around my neck.

Through a side yard, around another godforsaken fountain, and then crashing through a stand of banana trees, I finally see the road up ahead. With a final burst of energy, I jump the low wrought iron fence, almost fall, then catch myself thanks to a bank of ivy that leads down to the street.

My driver is still out front, and I barrel toward the car. He sees me and opens the back door as I run up. I put Evie inside as terrified partygoers rush through the Garden District yards.

"Drive. Now!" I jump in beside Evie, and when I close the door, I see Charles standing just inside the gate to Beau's home.

"Jesus, just look at that pasty-faced terminator."

He stares as we drive away, his face a stone mask of utter hatred.

Once we're jetting onto a main thoroughfare, free from anyone following us, I turn back to Evie. "I'm going to kill that motherfucker."

She's pale, so pale I can see the veins along her throat.

"Evie."

"You're alive. How? He stabbed you. I thought ..." Her voice breaks. "I thought he'd killed you. I thought I'd never see you again."

For so long, I thought I didn't have a heart. I mean, obviously I have one in my chest, the literal one. But I thought there was something missing, like I couldn't feel the way everyone else did. But now I know that's not true. Because the way she says those words, the anguish in her voice at the thought of me dying—fuck, I'm in love. I'm in love with this woman, and I don't know what to do with that.

"I'm okay." I reach inside my jacket and pull out the now-ruined iPad, the knife jutting from it. "See?"

"Thank god." She puts her palm to my cheek. "Lucius?"

"Yes?" I kiss her palm right as she doubles over and hurls the entire contents of her stomach onto the back floorboard.

24

EVIE

I wake. I know something's off. Like I'm in the wrong place. My eyes open, and I realize I'm in a strange bed without a stitch of clothing on my body.

Bolting upright, I snatch the blanket to my chest and try to get my bearings.

"You're at—"

I scream and strike out with the palm of my hand.

"Ow, hey!" Lucius rolls onto his back and grabs his nose. "Holy shit."

"Where am I?" I scoot to the edge of the bed and look around.

Stark lines, minimalist furniture, a fantastic view of the woods outside the window. "I'm at your place."

"Why would you go for my nose?" He groans.

I take a breath and shake off the fear. I'm safe. A weird laugh bubbles out of me.

"You think it's funny?"

"I think it's funny that I'm in your angular tower of terror, but somehow I feel safe."

He drops his hand, and I realize he's shirtless. A large bruise spreads across his chest right over his heart, the tangled vine tattoos emanating out from the spot of my bullet's impact. For a tiny second, I almost feel guilty. But then I remember Lucius definitely had it coming.

"What kind of idiot comes at someone who has a loaded gun pointed at their chest?" I blurt.

"First you attack my beautiful nose, and now you question my intelligence? Do you always wake up in this mood?" He tucks his hands behind his head, giving me a full view of his toned chest and abs.

I look away, and I swear to god I wish I could figure out how to stop myself from blushing. I can't, so I try to switch gears before he notices. "And why am I naked?" I remember a few details of what happened in the car, but then it's a blur. "What did you do to me?"

"Do you want the long or short version?" He reaches over and grabs my arm, gently pulling me back down onto the bed. "Just lie here. I'm not going to attack you until you ask nicely."

I roll my eyes. "Long version. I want play by play of your depravity."

He turns toward me and props himself on his elbow. I should be demanding my clothes, threatening him, running out of here, or calling for help. Instead,

I'm staring up at him and his five o'clock shadow, wondering what it would feel like against my skin.

"Let's see. First you threw up all over my favorite dress shoes."

"I recall that."

"Very rude of you." He gives me a surly look, then continues, "And after that, you did some dry heaving. Gut wrenching, if I'm being honest. Hurt me to hear it." He winces. "And after your stomach decided it was really and truly empty, you passed out."

"That's weird." I shake my head, my movement stirring up the scent of his sheets. That piney-citrusy smell of his mixed with fabric softener. Inexplicably delightful, if *I'm* being honest. "I'm not the passing out sort. I mean, yes, I was frightened and probably in some sort of shock, but still ..."

"Did anyone give you anything at the party? I was watching you most of the time and didn't see anything like that." He looks down at me with those light blue eyes, the ones that shouldn't belong to a devil like him. But the part that makes me come undone is the worry in them. Worry for *me*.

"Wait. I had some champagne. Not much though. Beau gave it to me." An image of him with blood pouring from his throat flashes in my mind.

"He must've drugged you. Something to make you more pliable? I don't know." He reaches across me and grabs his phone from the nightstand.

"What are you doing?"

"Calling our family doctor. I want him to check you."

"I'm fine." I put my hand on his.

"But we have no idea what he gave you."

"Lucius." I take his phone and return it to the nightstand. "I'm fine." When I look back at him, his eyes have gone to where the sheet is draped across my breasts.

That one look seems to set my skin ablaze, sparks rippling and eddying to that one electric spot between my thighs.

I clear my throat. "So I was drugged. That makes sense. At least it made my foot stop hurting." I wiggle my toes.

"I'm afraid that one's on me. I cleaned up the wound again and gave you a few shots of Novocain every few hours while you slept. Made you comfortable."

"You just have random Novocain on hand?"

He shrugs. "I had the doc swing by and deliver the little syringes. No big deal."

"You called your private doctor in the middle of the night to bring you Novocain syringes so I could sleep more comfortably?"

"In case you haven't noticed, Evie, I can't stop myself when it comes to you. I even brushed your teeth while you were out. No easy feat, but you know I'm not a quitter. Honestly, I'd do anything for you."

I glance down at the bruise on his chest. "Except die."

"I might do that too, if circumstances permit." He takes my hand and places it on his chest. "I've never wanted to protect anyone the way I want to protect you." He gives me a half-smile. "But given the way you just cracked my nose, I get the feeling you're pretty good at protecting yourself."

"I've worked on not being a victim ever again." I sigh. "But I guess I need to take more self-defense classes. I just ... Charles came up behind me and grabbed me, and I couldn't do anything. I couldn't save myself. You have no idea how frustrating that is."

"He's twice your size, Evie, and he had the element of surprise."

"I hate ..." I shouldn't be telling him any of this. But with the morning sun filtering through his wide windows and draping across his body like a warm blanket, I feel so open. Vulnerable. No one has ever known me, but that's by design. I couldn't let anyone get close. My life has far too many secrets, too many dark corners, and absolutely too many ghosts.

"What's going on in here?" He runs his fingertips along my forehead.

I meet his gaze, the way he looks at me melting me from the inside. "I was just saying I hate to feel helpless. The last time I felt that way ..." I can't finish the thought out loud. It means too much and carries too much weight. Because Lucius is part of the reason I've never been able to open up to anyone. Not just because of what he did to Red, but because I'd wanted him so badly in my extravagant teenage fantasies. He'd colored every aspect of my early life, and then he'd destroyed everything. Blasted away the parts of me that kept me bound to this place, to these people, to the horrors of the Acquisition.

"I get it. The last time you felt helpless was when I killed your—"

I lean up and kiss him, taking the sting of that statement away before he can complete it.

He answers, pressing me down onto the pillow as his mouth takes mine in a vehement kiss, one that blurs the lines between lust and love. Because in this moment I realize, I *do* love him in a way that's as confusing as it is real. It's desire, it's nostalgia, it's longing, it's so many emotions wrapped in a tight bundle. He's been at the center of that bundle all along. In my nightmares and wildest dreams—it's always been him.

How long have I loved him? Even when he killed Red? Even then? The thought horrifies me but also rings true. Maybe I've never let anyone get close because I didn't want just anyone. I wanted this devil with the angel eyes. I want his love, and I have to give him mine. He demands it of me—when he protects me, when he saves me, when he risks everything for me. That revelation is like some sort of bomb that detonates through me. I'm the same, yet not. Evie,

Evelyn, whoever I'll become—I'm someone who knows love, and that's all anyone can ever truly hope for, isn't it?

When he climbs on top of me, I realize he's naked beneath the sheet.

I grip his shoulders, my nails digging in as he rests between my thighs.

Pulling back from the kiss, he cups my cheek. "Is this what you want?"

"What?"

"I want you to be sure, Evie. Because once we do this, I'm never letting you go. I've waited my whole life for you. I just didn't realize it. Not until you shot me through the heart."

"That's a lot of pretty words from a vicious Vinemont." My eyes water as I look up at him.

He nips at my bottom lip. "Fewer then? In that case, I'll make it simple. I love you, Evie."

How can this be real? How can we both have taken such long, twisted roads and arrived at the same place? I don't know the answer to that. I probably never will.

"Love? From the devil?"

"Such as it is. It's yours."

Warmth suffuses my skin, lighting me up as I stare into his eyes. "I shouldn't. I tried not to. I fought it so hard." A tear leaks from my eye, and he catches it on his fingertip. "But I ... I think I love you, too."

For a moment, he looks surprised. Why does that

seem both heartbreaking and adorable at the same time?

"You do?"

"Yes."

"Even though I—"

"Shh." I press my finger to his lips. "We only talk about the future, okay? The future is where we go from here, not back. That's the only way this can work."

He smiles and nuzzles his nose against mine. "I like the sound of that." He shifts, and his cock grazes against my pussy. "Fuck, I love the *feel* of that."

I wrap my arms around his neck and kiss him. He devours me, his tongue caressing mine as he runs his hands down my body. When he cups my breast, I moan at the pressure as he squeezes.

"Fuck, you're going to make me bust just from touching you." He groans and kisses down my throat, his lips so warm against my skin yet sending out goosebumps all the same.

I move my hips against him, and he grabs my waist. "Don't." His voice is low and raw as he licks my nipple.

His touch sends sparks of heat dancing through me, and I need more, but he won't let me move. Instead, he holds me down and sucks my breasts, his tongue wicked and nimble. By the time he moves lower, I'm a desperate mess, my hands in his hair, my back arching as he drops kisses down my stomach.

When he gets to my pussy, he yanks the blankets off and stares down at me. He's so tense, his hard cock at attention as he runs his thumbs along my lips, spreading me open. It's filthy and hot, and I moan when he leans closer and his breath dances across my hot, wet skin.

"Look at that pretty little cunt." He grins and buries his face between my thighs.

"Lucius!" I gasp as he places his palms against my inner thighs and pushes, spreading me open wide as he licks, a groan in his throat.

He presses his tongue inside me and squeezes my thighs, and I think I might combust from the sensation of being held open and plundered.

But then he moves to my clit, sucking it between his lips then lashing it with his tongue. I grind on him, using his face as he teases and tastes. Sliding two fingers inside me, he looks up. "You need more, Evie. You need so much more." He returns to my clit, flicking the tip of his tongue against it as I shudder with need.

"Please."

"Please?" He crawls up my body and shares my taste with me, his mouth hot and wet against mine.

He notches his cock at my entrance, and his thick head presses inside me.

I can't stop this, not for anything. Maybe this was always in our stars. I don't know, but I'm certain I need Lucius like I need my next breath.

"So goddamn tight." He groans and presses deeper, his cock sliding in my wetness as I urge him deeper.

"Don't stop."

"Stopping has never been an option when it comes to you, darling." He runs one hand behind my back and clamps down on my shoulder. Holding me in place, he slides the rest of the way inside, his hips thrusting in a smooth movement.

I'm full of him. Full of love for him. I never want this to end.

He pulls back and surges forward again, his hand still holding me in place as he moves. "Made for me. Jesus Christ." He groans and pulls out quickly, then plunges deep, starting a fast rhythm.

I open my legs wider for him, my heels in the air as our bodies slap together, the sound ricocheting around the room. I press my hands against the headboard, and he releases my shoulder, pulling back as he keeps pistoning inside me.

"Look at you. Just fucking look at you." He cups my breasts and pinches my nipples as he works my pussy.

I arch at his touch, my body alight inside and out.

"Fuck yes, take it all, Evie. I want to see every inch of me inside you." He leans back even more, his gaze on where his cock slides in and out of me. "Ah, fuck." His cock hardens even more, and he falls on top of me, his mouth finding mine in a messy, frantic kiss.

Our bodies, slicked with sweat, slide against each other as we learn each other, taste each other.

"What do you need, darling?" He bites my ear, then sucks my neck. "I want you to get off so hard you see stars. Tell me what this pretty pussy needs."

I moan at his words, at all the sensations that rocket through me with each of his strokes.

"I know what you need, my little Evie." He moves one hand between us as he stares down at me, his dark hair wild and his gaze never wavering.

When he presses his thumb to my clit and starts stroking it, I rake my nails down his back. "Lucius, yes!"

"That's my good girl." He reclaims one of my nipples in his mouth, biting harder this time. The hint of pain sends my arousal spiraling even higher, and I can't stop the rising wave of euphoria that's rushing toward me.

"I—I ..." My breath is stolen away as my orgasm hits. It comes from somewhere deep inside, a release that rolls on and on as I claw at Lucius and cry his name. He doesn't stop stroking me, his mouth on my tits, on my throat. I come until I can barely breathe, my body spent and so sensitive.

"That was so fucking hot." He runs his palm down my chest, between my breasts, and then to my pussy. "God, feel that. Feel how perfect." He takes my hand and brings it to his cock as he thrusts in and out.

It's so filthy, so goddamn perfect to feel his hard cock sliding into my wet pussy.

"All for you, Evie. Every bit of me is yours." He pulls out, then flips me over onto my stomach.

With a hard pull, he yanks me onto his dick. I squeal at the pressure when he enters me from behind.

"Fuck yes." He runs a finger down my ass and strokes the hole.

"Lucius!" I turn to look at him.

He smirks back at me and applies pressure, slipping the tip of his finger inside. "I'm going to take every hole you have, darling. I can promise you that. Maybe not right now." He pushes it farther, and I can't stifle my moan. How can something so wrong feel so good? It sends so much arousal flooding through me that I swear I get even wetter.

"You like that?" He grunts, and his animalistic manner only turns me on more. When he slaps my ass, I jump. "I asked you a question, Evie. Do you like it when I play with your tight asshole?"

"Yes," I breathe.

"I know you do, good girl." He reaches up with his other hand and takes a handful of hair.

When he thrusts inside me again, I arch and take every bit of him. He pulls my hair, riding me while he fingers my asshole.

I'm so worked up, so turned on, I feel that wave inside me again. It rolls and rolls, and when Lucius plunges his finger even deeper, I cry out and come again. This one's deeper and shorter, but no less powerful.

"I can feel you, Evie. Your cunt wants to milk me." He thrusts so hard the bed shakes. "Take it." His cock kicks, and I feel his release spurting inside me. "Take it all like a good girl."

My orgasm crests again in a final burst of bliss. It leaves me a boneless mess as I sink down into the bed. His come leaks down my inner thighs, but I don't care. Not when I've just been fucked into two delicious orgasms.

He leans over my back and presses a kiss between my shoulder blades. "Good girl."

Why does that stupid phrase make me go all weak? I should protest, should tear him down and inform him I'm not a dog. But the way he says it, god! The gritty way he praises me as he gives me pleasure and takes his own—I already crave it.

And I let him come inside me. I groan.

"What?" He falls beside me and pulls me to him.

"We just—"

"Lived out our rage-sex dreams with each other?" he fills in.

"Went bareback," I correct.

"Yeah. I know. But—" He takes my chin and pulls me to face him. "There was no way I was going to pull out. Not with you. Not with us."

"I'm on birth control."

"Okay."

I squint. "Okay?"

"Yeah." He is completely at ease. Smug almost.

"Like it doesn't matter to you either way?"

"It doesn't. Look, I'm locked in here, Evie. You and me. I told you before we got down to business that this is forever."

"What if I don't *want* you to be my forever?"

He laughs, the sound low and so damn sexy. "Of course you do. Just look at me."

"God, I'm right back to wanting to punch you." I start to scoot away from him, but he doesn't let me go.

"You can punch me as long as you don't leave me." He runs his fingers through my hair. "Your roots are showing. I love that color. And you have it down below to matc—"

"Honestly!" I wrinkle my nose.

"What?" He kisses my wrinkled nose. "I like it."

Could this be real? Am I lying here with the man I wanted to kill—and will probably still want to kill from time to time—actually having a conversation about a real future?

I sigh and relax onto him, his heart thumping powerfully beneath my cheek. "You really want children?"

"With you? Yeah."

"What if this is just a passing fascination because of—"

"No." He pulls me up his body until we're eye-to-eye. "I've never been surer of anything in my life."

My eyes water, and I feel so damn exposed. Like a creature without a shell.

"Hey." He kisses me softly, warmly—in a way I thought he wasn't capable of. "I'm sure of you, Evie. I'm an asshole, a fucking deviant. I know that. I've always known it. But you are my downfall. You make me want to be more than a fucked-up monster. Not saying I can be, but you're the only one who's ever convinced me to try. All right?"

I nod and kiss him back, because for once, I'm not alone.

And for once, I don't want to be.

25

EVIE

"What now?" I sip my coffee as Lucius, shirtless and with his pajama pants slung low, tries to make breakfast.

"Now, food." He cracks an egg into the pan, but some bits of eggshell make it in. He opens the trash can to dump the whole thing, but the egg is stuck to the pan.

"Shit." He jiggles it, trying to get it to come off, but it doesn't. I grin behind my coffee cup. He tosses the pan into the sink and grabs another from beneath the stove.

"I take it you don't cook much?" I stand and walk over to him. I'm wearing one of his button-up shirts with nothing underneath.

"I can cook." He stares at the stove as if he's trying to remember test answers. "I've made macaroni and cheese plenty of times, not to mention peanut butter and jellies."

"Impressive."

He gives me a sideways glance. "Your sarcasm is noted and ignored."

"Sit down." I point with the spatula.

"What? You know how to cook? I thought you were career woman extraordinaire, out to tear apart businesses and put them back together."

I walk to the fridge and look inside. Neat, orderly, barely touched. Grabbing some butter, I return to the stove and take the fresh pan, put in a pat, and turn the flame to medium.

He comes up behind me and puts his hands on my hips beneath the long shirt.

"Watch and learn." Once the butter is melted, I crack an egg one-handed.

"Amazing." He moves my hair to the side and kisses the back of my neck. "Show me more."

I crack another egg, then salt and pepper them.

Lucius pulls the collar of his shirt to the side and kisses along my shoulder. His touch, the simple press of his lips against my skin, sends heat rushing across my skin.

"Over medium." He nibbles my ear. "Please."

When he sinks to his knees behind me, I try to turn. He stops me and then kisses up the backs of my thighs.

I make a strangled sound when he spreads my legs.

"Lucius, I don't think—" I gasp when he licks me from the back.

"Shh, I'm having breakfast." He spreads my cheeks and licks me from front to back, his tongue going places no man has touched. I lean over the stove, the eggs sizzling lightly as Lucius presses two fingers inside me.

"Mmm, you're still wet. Good girl." He licks my asshole, focusing on the sensitive skin.

I moan and try to watch the eggs, but when he moves his slick fingers to my clit, I throw my head back. "Lucius!"

He sucks my skin, his mouth hot and wet on my ass as his fingers strum my clit.

I'm shaking, my entire body focused on his mouth, his fingers, *him*.

"I'm no cook, but perhaps you should flip them?" His voice is muffled, and he lifts one of my legs all the way up until my foot is on the countertop. "Oh, yes, darling," he practically purrs. "I like this view quite a lot."

I flip the eggs. Barely.

He strokes me faster, both fingers giving me the friction I need. His tongue at the back is sending me higher and higher. The toaster pops up right as I come on a whine, my thighs shaking as my hips lock. He doesn't stop, and I can feel him groan against my hot skin.

When my orgasm finally subsides, I pull my foot from the counter.

He tries to push it back.

"The eggs."

"Fuck the eggs." He kisses my cheeks, then bites my ass.

"You're the devil!" I turn off the stove.

He rises and goes to the sink, cleaning up and then grabbing two plates and the toast. I add the eggs, and he takes my hand and pulls me over to the counter.

"These look amazing, though I've already seen the most delicious sight this morning." He takes a bite of his toast.

"I don't even know what to say." I don't. I'm actually embarrassed about how much I liked what he just did.

"I ate your ass and now I'm eating your eggs." He motions toward my plate. "They're very good. Thank you."

I shake my head and take a bite. He's right. My eggs are perfect.

"This is surreal." I drink my coffee slowly.

"What? Good eggs?"

"Us."

"Already doubting?" he teases.

"Not doubting, just adjusting, I guess. I never imagined any of this. I mean, if I'm being honest, this is so far outside of my realm of possibilities that it's almost laughable."

"I'll make you a believer, Evie."

"I already believe. In you." I lean over and kiss his cheek.

"Good." He picks up my toast and feeds it to me. "Eat. I need you full of energy for my next venture inside you."

"I have work to do. Not to mention, we need to talk about last night. They aren't going to go away just because Beau's dead. They'll find someone else to try and resurrect the entire machine."

"I know." He pulls my chair closer to his. "But that doesn't sound anywhere near as fun as what I have planned for you."

"And what is that?" I meet his gaze.

"I figured we could start with a little spanking and—"

"Why? What did you do wrong?"

His lips twitch. "The spanking is for *you*, little Evie."

I wish that didn't make my heart beat faster, but it does. "You need to focus. First things first: that psycho Charles. I mean, he doesn't care about rules. He killed the Sovereign —his uncle—without a second thought. He'll probably do the same to us once he finds us."

"I'll track him down. I have plenty of contacts for that." He waves my concerns away. "Now back to the spanking. First I'm going to—"

A sound chimes on his phone. His eyes widen.

"What?" I turn to follow his gaze.

"Where the fuck have you been?" A man's voice

booms through the house. "I've been calling and texting. You better be dead."

"Shit." Lucius stands and keeps me behind him.

I tense, because I know that voice, and I know the man attached to it.

Sinclair walks around the corner and into the kitchen.

Then he stops, his harsh gaze going right to me. The hate in his eyes is almost a palpable touch, and he grits out, "What. The. Fuck?"

26

LUCIUS

"The Sovereign is dead." I figure if I lead with that, it might stave off the chances of Sin going nuclear.

"I'm aware." He stalks over to us. "We need to talk." He glances at Evie over my shoulder. "Alone."

"That's fine. I was just leaving." She turns.

I take her hand. "No, you weren't. And you can stay."

"No," she and Sin say in unison.

"Yes, you should go." Sin looks down his nose at her.

"Stop." I step between them.

"I have work to do." She pulls her hand from mine—because I let her. "And I need to get dressed."

"Too bad you don't have any clothes."

"I'll make do," she calls as she disappears into my bedroom.

"I warned you." Sin glowers. "I told you not to do this."

"When have I ever listened to you?"

"That's your fucking problem." He turns and walks to the window. "You do things without thinking, and then I have to clean up your mess."

"You don't have to do shit." I cross my arms over my chest. "I know what I'm doing. I know—"

"She's an enemy!" he yells. "For all you know, she could be working with these assholes and just getting close to you so she can put a knife in your back."

"That's not what this is."

"Oh, is that right?" He spins and meets my gaze. "Is this love? Is that what you think? Does she love you, little brother? Have you told her about your addictions, about how much you enjoy hurting people, about all the shit you've done that can never be erased?"

"You're crossing a line." I flex my sore fists.

"Good! Maybe you'll wake the fuck up. She's trying to steal our family business right out from under us. She got a special invitation to party with the people who'd like nothing better than to see us all dead. And that's including my *children*!"

"I would never let anyone hurt them." I stride to him until we're toe to toe. "You know I'd never jeopardize the kids."

"Do I? You're fucking someone who tried to kill you. Who *almost* succeeded."

The front door opens again, my security system

beeping, and Teddy bounds up the stairs. "I'm supposed to be on rotations so this better be—" He stops when he sees us. "Okay, so what's wrong?"

"What's wrong is our brother thinks pussy is more important than family."

"She's not just pussy." I grit my teeth. "Don't talk about her like that."

Sin smirks, his dark blue eyes lighting with malice. "Or what?"

"Guys, don't do this." Teddy holds both his hands up as he comes closer.

"Do what?" Sin cracks his neck. "Tell Lucius the truth about his foolish conquest?"

Teddy cocks his head to the side. "So you and Evie are—"

"Together," I finish for him.

"Even though she—"

"Shot me. Yes."

Teddy scrubs a hand down his face. "Whoa."

"He's putting his dick feels over his family name." Sin shakes his head slowly. "Was getting your dick wet worth it? Was she good, Lucius? I bet she was, since she brought you to your knees."

"Stop talking about her." Anger simmers inside me, already on the edge of boiling over. "I won't warn you again."

"Oh shit," Teddy says under his breath.

Sin gives me a vicious half-grin. "Stop talking about the conniving little bitch who wants—"

I shove him backwards. He expected the move and comes off the window with his fists flying.

"Not again!" Teddy backs away.

Sin tackles me to the floor, my back sliding with an ugly squeak against the cold tile. "You can't go five seconds without fucking up!" He punches me hard, my jaw exploding with pain.

"You need to back the fuck off!" I yell right back and shove him off, then get to my feet.

He's up too, and he takes off his jacket and tosses it at Teddy.

"Guys, please."

"Shut up, Teddy," Sin and I say in unison.

"Come on." I motion Sin forward. "You want to get fucked up? I'm happy to oblige."

"You're still the little brother. Don't forget." He comes for me, his long reach almost giving him a glass jaw shot on me. But I dance out of his reach, then propel myself forward, nailing him in the gut with one fist. When he doubles over slightly, I bring my knee up into his face.

"Fuck!" He yowls and dances back, blood running from his nose. "You piece of shit!" He runs at me, trying to wrestle me to the ground, but I tangle with him and shove him off.

He staggers back toward the window. "I guess her pussy was the best you ever had for you to be such a whipped piece of sh—"

Two things happen at once.

One, Teddy yells no.

Two, I charge Sin, and we both hurtle toward the window. For a moment, it only trembles. After all, it's not plain glass. But then the full force of our impact rattles across it, and with a sharp crack, it shatters under the brute force. We both tumble out onto the lawn one story below.

The breath is knocked out of me, and my side aches where I hit the turf. But I get up. I always get back to my feet. It's the only way to win a fight.

Sin is up, too, his breathing labored as he feels along his left shin.

"Broken?" I ask.

"It will be once I ram it up your ass."

"Come on then." I bring my fists up.

"Sin! Lucius! Stop!" Teddy rushes out the door and runs to us. "Just stop!"

"I'll stop when this asshole comes to his senses." Sin brings up his fists, too, and we start circling each other.

"Then this won't end until one of you is dead." Teddy, the only peacemaker in the entire Vinemont family tree, sighs long-sufferingly.

"So be it." I thumb my nose and dart forward, jabbing in Sin's face.

He knocks my fist away and aims a kick right to my thigh.

"Fuck!" I yell and back up.

Sin turns until his back is to the sun, taking the

advantage. "Come on, little brother. Take your medicine."

I take a deep breath and put my hands on my hips. "You're right."

Sin arches a brow. "I know."

I shake my head and take in big gulps of air. The pain in my side and thigh are dull stabs of a rusted blade.

Sin drops his fists slowly and approaches. "She's just a piece of ass. A dangerous one. That's why you want her."

"Mmm." I suck in air between my teeth.

"Good, let's de-escalate." Teddy claps. "Come on, I can patch you two up inside."

Sin comes closer.

That's all it takes. I spring forward, tackling him to the grass with a bone-jarring thud. He fights back, swinging and struggling. He gets in some hard hits, but then he fucks up. He turns over to get up. I jump on his back and wrap my forearm around his windpipe.

"Get the fuck off!" He yanks at my arm and tries to get to his feet. I knee him in the back of the legs and drag him down, pinning him as he fights.

"Guys!" Teddy moves closer. "Come on."

"Don't say another shit word about Evie." I squeeze harder.

"Fuck ... you," Sin grits out.

I add the leverage of my other arm, pulling on my

wrist and completely cutting his air flow. "You had your chance."

He fights even harder, but I can tell his energy is waning. No air will do that to anyone.

"Lucius!" Teddy taps my back. "He's done. Let him go."

"He better be done." I release my hold and back away from him. He's dangerous on a good day. Right now? He might try to take my head off with his bare hands.

Teddy moves between us again, his hands out, as Sin gets back to his feet.

His face is red, his clothing covered in grass stains.

"Can we stop this stupid shit and talk about what happened last night?" Teddy looks at me, then Sin. Back and forth.

"I'm happy to talk." I shrug despite the pain in my side.

Sin stays silent for a while, his gaze sizing me up. He may be preparing for another attack. I keep my knees slightly bent, ready to clap back if I need to.

Finally, he walks past me, his shoulder crashing against mine. "Let's go inside."

"You're paying for the window. It was custom." I follow him as Teddy brings up the rear.

"Take it out of my pay. Like I give a fuck." Sin takes the stairs two at a time and goes to the coffeemaker in the kitchen.

I hurry past him and check my bedroom and bathroom. No Evie. When I come back out, Teddy hitches a thumb over his shoulder. "She took the Lambo."

"What?" I peer out the busted window but don't see my blue Diablo anywhere.

"Gone. You would've noticed if you'd been having a normal conversation like brothers. Instead, you were playing *Super Smash Brothers* on the front lawn." Teddy heads to the fridge and scoops out ice into some Ziploc bags. He hands one to each of us.

"*Super Smash Brothers*?" Sin presses his bag to his nose.

"Fighting game. Nintendo." Teddy leans over to inspect my side. "You'll have another bruise to match the one on your chest. You may have broken a rib. Won't know for sure without imaging."

"Not a chance." I tuck the ice pack under my arm, the cold stinging my hot skin.

Sin leans against the counter and sips his coffee, his eyes on me. "Since Evie is gone for the moment ..."

I can tell he wants to say some shit, so I straighten. I will kick his ass as many times as necessary for him to respect my woman. Even though she's gone. Even though she took my favorite car and didn't say a word to me as she left. Not a wise move on her part. That psycho bastard Beau will come after her, if not the whole crew of Acquisition fans.

"Right. Evie is gone," Teddy prompts.

Sin nods and continues carefully, "I want you to tell me everything that happened last night."

"Umm, someone send me the notes later." Teddy's looking at his phone. "I've got to get back to the hospital."

"Family dinner at home tomorrow night," Sin calls as Teddy hurries down the stairs. "That goes for you, too." He glares at me.

"Again?"

"Stella is making that pork tenderloin, the one everyone raves about."

"Oh, shit. With the mashed potatoes? I'm there."

"Glad we have that sorted out." His tone is utterly taciturn. "Now tell me where the fuck you were all night and what happened at that party."

"I can do better than that." I walk into my office to grab the iPad I'd stolen from the greeter. "I've got the names of everyone at that shitty soiree. We can wipe them out for good."

When I open the top drawer of my desk, it has the usual pens, liquor, stale cigarettes, and sticky notes. But no iPad. A sinking sensation creeps into my gut, and I open the other drawers. The iPad isn't here.

Fuck.

27

EVIE

My apartment is quiet. I creep in, my head on a swivel. The gun I took from Lucius's nightstand is steady in my hand as I sweep the entire place. No one's here.

I hurry back to my front door and change the code on the lock, then flip every deadbolt I have. When that's done, I can finally let myself breathe again.

Leaning against the door, I try to put the jumbled night back together, to look for a way out of all this. But my mind goes back to one place. Lucius. A pang of guilt tries to take over. I stole his car, and—I turn the iPad over in my hands—I stole the one thing he wanted from that hellish scene last night.

I couldn't leave it with him. Not when he could be playing me to get closer to the Acquisition. I have that stupid part of me, the one down deep, that believes he was being honest with me. That he *loves* me. *And you said you loved him*, my thoughts whisper.

All a ruse on his part. The same game a cat plays before it goes in for the kill. That's all I am to Lucius. So why doesn't it *feel* like a game?

"Ugh." I drop onto my sofa and inspect the iPad. The screen is busted, sliced through when Beau tried to filet Lucius. Can it even be saved? I turn it over. The backside is dented, and the only thing that kept the knife from going all the way through was the metal case.

I shiver when I remember Beau's arm around me, his hot breath on my neck. That's twice Lucius has saved me from that big bastard. I glance at my door again. It's strong, reinforced. Could Beau still get through it somehow?

I need to shower, to wash off the scent of Lucius. As I decide to do just that, I reach down and pull the fabric of his shirt up to my nose and inhale. Even though I've escaped, he's still all around me.

Flipping the iPad back over, I try to power it on. Nothing happens. I didn't expect it to. I'll have to find someone who can get into it and pull that guest list—along with whatever treasures might lie within—for me. The sooner I know who I'm up against, the better. Those people will be coming after me now. They saw me leave with their number one enemy. I'll never be safe.

I take the iPad into my room and to the back of my closet. My gun safe is in here. I used to actually keep my pistol in it, but ever since I came back to town, my gun's been staying in my bag or under my pillow. It'll be a good hiding spot for the iPad, even though my place is already locked up like Fort Knox.

Once I've stowed the iPad, I finally pull off Lucius's shirt. I stay strong and toss it in the top of my hamper instead of smelling it again.

Showers are the best of times and the worst of times. I can stand under the spray and think about all the things I need to do, solve some problems, come up with new strategies, or I'll remember all the things I've done wrong, the people I've lost, and as always, I'll think of Lucius. How many times have I plotted his death while lathering up? A million. But now, I don't think of that at all. I think of his life, of the future he talked about with me.

I keep telling myself it wasn't real, that I need to stop being so naïve. But, when I left, he'd been fighting his brother. For me. Something I never imagined.

After too much time rinsing and thinking, I finally step out and wrap myself in a towel. When I walk into my bedroom, I stop dead.

"Hey darlin'. I don't think we were finished with our talk." Lucius reclines on my bed, his shirt off and his hands clasped behind his head. "And with the way you left, I'm thinking you're spooked. Maybe you're wondering if I'm playing you? Something along those lines? Am I warm?"

I clutch my towel to my chest, my mouth open but no words coming out. Then my thoughts finally get traction. "How the hell did you get in here?"

"If I told you, wouldn't that ruin the surprise?"

I stare at him. All of him. His broad chest and well-toned muscles. God, of course I worshipped him when I was a teenager. Even though he's over thirty now, he's still got everything right where it counts. Not to mention the things he can do with his tongue. I press my thighs together at the thought.

His gaze tracks the movement, then returns to my eyes. "When I was here last time, I took the liberty of having my locksmith come out and—"

"You're fucking kidding me." I stomp toward the bed, then stop when I realize I'm too close to him. Too naked, and he's far too appealing with his hungry eyes and taut body.

"Not kidding. He even programmed your digital lock code into my phone." He pulls it up from beside him on the bed and shows me. "See? Even if you change the code, it'll still transmit it right to me. So there's no point trying to run back here and hide from me, Evie."

"I'm not hiding."

"Seems like it. You snuck out and took a little something of mine."

I walk around the bed to my dresser. "It wasn't yours to begin with." When I toss a look over my shoulder, I see an ugly bruise forming on his right side. "What happened?"

"Fell out a window with a bear. You should see the bear."

"So, your brother."

"You missed it?" he asks. "The whole thing?"

"I was busy."

"Stealing the iPad. Yeah, I suppose you were." He rolls toward me and props up on his elbow. "You really just ditched me." He gives a wolf's smile. "Cold, Evie."

"Not cold. Just logical."

"How so?"

"You have a reputation. I assumed once you got what you wanted from me, you'd move on."

"What else do you think you know about me?"

"You've been in so many fights you've probably lost count." I gesture toward the smattering of scars on his torso. "You've killed people. You've done horrible things. You drink too much. You hide behind wit and brutality."

He pins me with his gaze, his eyes so clear. "I don't hide with you."

How does he break me down with one simple statement?

"I'm all the things you said. And I don't know if I can change any of it. But I know I can be there for you.

I *want* to be someone different—no, not different—" He chews his bottom lip. "Better. I meant better, for you. But by the same token, I will hunt, hurt, and slaughter anyone who comes for you." He sits up and swings his legs off the side of the bed. "You never should've left my place. It's not safe out here."

"Don't you realize I'm not safe there either?" I throw my hands up.

His gaze drifts down to where I have my towel tied over my breasts, then he meets my gaze again. "Come here." He says it with command, but also a gentleness that soothes my worried heart.

I sigh and step toward him.

He reaches out and grabs the towel, pulling it away and tossing it to the floor. Running his hands along my hips, he looks up at me, then kisses my stomach, his lips leaving a trail of fire as they drift lower.

"Lucius." I try to step back, but he holds me in place.

"If you run from me, I'll follow you." He kisses my pussy, his touch so soft, almost reverent. "I'll find you, Evie. Every time. I warned you what would happen. Remember?" He delves his tongue between my lips, and I shiver, my nipples tightening almost painfully.

I remember. He said forever. "Yes."

"I meant every word." Another lick.

I grab his hair.

"I know you've probably been thinking of a million

reasons why this can't happen. Maybe you think I'm playing you to save Magnolia. Or maybe something equally wrong—like trying to find the Acquisition assholes. Those things are just bonuses. In the grand scheme, they will fall into place with or without the two of us being right here, right now. But you and me?" He kisses me again, open-mouthed, his tongue sliding farther along my clit. "We're real. No lies, no reasons to be together except for one." He leans back and looks up at me. "Now sit on my face so I can prove how much I love you."

"Oh my god." I groan as he lies back and pulls me with him, settling me on top of him.

"More." He mumbles against me as he licks and sucks all the right places.

I move my hips, already chasing my orgasm as his magic tongue caresses me, his fingers digging into my hips as he pulls me down onto him. I push back a little.

"Evie, if you don't smother me to death, I don't want you on top of me." He yanks my hips down, the contact so intense that I squeal as his tongue sets my body on fire. It's electric, all-consuming. I grind against him shamelessly, my body taking over as I work my pussy all over his mouth.

He doesn't stop, his tongue focusing just right, my clit throbbing then getting that magical feeling of being so hot and tender. And then I explode, my orgasm shooting up high into the sky, shattering, and raining down like sparks. I come hard, my body surrendering as Lucius plays me with his tongue, his mouth. He gives me everything, and I take it, rolling my hips until the orgasm finally recedes.

I climb off him and flop onto the bed.

He licks his lips, his mouth still wet.

"I guess you love me a lot?" I can't help but smile.

"Enough to die happily right between your thighs."

He takes my hand and puts it over his heart. "I can't get enough of you. I already want more."

"If you do that again, I'm going to be the one who dies." I bury my face in the bed.

"I'll have to mark it on the itinerary for later. In the meantime, what do we have planned? I mean, I'll be taking the iPad, of course. But other than that, what's doing?"

"I'm not giving you the iPad." I turn my head so I can look at him.

"Why not?"

"Because in case you've forgotten, your brother came over to your place with his ass in a twist about me. Apparently, it led to you breaking a rib or two." I point at his side. "And if I just give up that computer, what's to stop him from wiping me out?"

"Sin will come around."

I blow a hair out of my face. "That's cute. Brotherly support and all. But I'm not risking my life on your warm assessment of your cold, calculating brother."

"Is that all you're worried about?" He rolls over again, and we're face to face.

"Yes. I mean, I'm also worried that you're just saying all these wonderful words and doing these things that, quite frankly, are likely illegal, to my body so that I'll back away from Magnolia. And I know you want to start fresh, like we don't have this immense, tragic history, but I don't know if that's really possible. Can two people who are so damaged ever make something like this work?"

"I love your eyes without the blue contacts. Brown eyes suit you. And you're not damaged. Your past is why you're strong. That's one of the few things I learned from my crazy-as-fuck mother. Her past destroyed her. But she used all her sorrow, rage, and heartbreak to teach Sin and me how to be strong. Her methods were fucked up, naturally, but I can say without hesitation that I'm a bad motherfucker because of her. Just like you're a bad bitch because of all the shit you went through. That's not damage. That's thriving despite shit conditions."

"See?" I shake my head. "You go and say things like that. Is it real?"

"It's real. And forget all that serious stuff…" He reaches out and runs his hand down my side, his gaze following. "Just look at the shape of you."

I can't let him get me off track. "I'm certain your brother doesn't think it's real."

He groans. "He's cockblocking me, and he isn't even

here." He scoots closer. "I think I have a solution for this."

"What's that?" I'm already leaning away from him, especially given how suspicious his glib tone is.

He reaches out and pulls me into his arms, making me laugh against my will. "I think it's time you meet the family."

28

LUCIUS

"This is a bad idea." Evie fidgets in the passenger seat.

"It's a great idea." I take her hand and kiss it.

"I don't know how I let you talk me into this."

"I do. How many orgasms was it? Five or six?"

"Exactly. You waited until I was incapacitated."

"I'm nothing if not a scoundrel." I shrug. "But maybe that's why you find me so lovable."

"Your sweet talking doesn't change the fact that your entire family hates me."

"They don't hate you."

She gives me a deadpan stare.

"Okay, maybe they don't understand you. They see you as an enemy."

"I *am* an enemy. I mean, I'm not giving up on Magnolia. Maybe I won't destroy it like I originally planned, but I'm going to streamline it whether you like it or not."

"So, don't lead with that." I glance at her. "Just table that for a while, and we can come back to it. You don't have to do a takeover to work your magic on the company. I can be persuaded to work with you in exchange for certain favors."

"I don't do sex work."

"You won't have to. I make sex more like a vacation than work." I lick between her fingers.

"You're the worst." She laughs.

"Agreed. But, like I said, might not want to bring Magnolia up tonight. A little more time and massaging are needed there."

"They're going to doubt me. They'll say this is too fast—because it *is*. I mean, I just tried to kill you, and now we're what? Dating?"

"We're in love." I nibble her knuckles.

"That sounds absolutely absurd."

"Doesn't mean it's not true."

"Okay, so what about …" She takes a deep breath as we enter the Vinemont gate. "What about Red?"

"You can talk as much or as little about that as you want. But just know, Stella suffered at his hands." Even now, I remember the hell he put her through. Tonight won't be easy, but it has to happen. Evie is part of my life now. A huge part. "She's not going to remember him fondly. None of us are."

"I know." She squeezes my hand. "I won't bring him up. Or, at least I'll try not to."

"I think that's all you can do. He's part of your life, and for good or ill, he was your brother. Nothing we can do to change it."

"When did you become so level-headed?"

"Don't worry. It'll pass. I'll be back to reckless in no time."

"I'd expect nothing less."

"There's only one thing I need you to remember for this entire evening."

"What's that?" She stares ahead as the house comes into view.

"That I've got your back."

"Against your family?" She doesn't sound convinced.

"You're part of that family now." I know it sounds so fucking insane and sudden. Or maybe it's neither of those. Maybe our stars have been aligned from the moment we came screaming into this world. I don't know. I just want her to trust me, to have faith that I'll protect her.

She takes a deep breath. "I can hold my own."

"Are you listening to my thoughts?" I pull up near the front porch.

"Maybe. I thought I heard some static back there at the gate." She shoots me a wicked glance.

"There's the spirit." I kiss her palm then kill the

engine and step from the car. As I walk around to help her out, little Teddy runs onto the porch.

"Hey!" He jumps from the top step, lands in a hunch, and does a forward roll to his feet.

"Wow." Evie takes my hand and steps out.

Teddy freezes, his eyes on Evie. I don't blame him. She's wearing a yellow sundress, the kind with those thin straps at the top. She's a bombshell.

"Teddy, this is my girlfriend Evie."

"Girlfriend?" She shoots me a look.

"What?" I pull her closer and wrap my arm around her waist.

"You have a girlfriend?" Teddy looks aghast.

"Yep."

"Does Mommy know?"

"She's about to find out."

"Okay." He turns to run inside, then stops. "Hey. Didn't you say a girl named Evie shot you?" His wide eyes go back to her.

"Sure did, champ. Isn't she something?" I kiss her cheek.

"I'm telling Mommy." He runs off as Evie groans.

We walk up the front steps.

"I've been here before."

"You have?" I stop on the porch, the sunset sending dappled rays through the trees at the edge of the lawn.

"When I was a kid, yeah. Red and I came over for some ceremonial thing. Maybe when your mom was Sovereign. I'm not sure."

"Was I here?"

"Yes." She looks down, her cheeks turning a light shade of pink.

"I wish I could remember it."

"You were already a teenager, way too cool for a little girl like me. But we did talk."

"We did?" I face her and run my fingers down a lock of her soft hair. "I bet I was charming."

"You were larger than life for me. The evil smile, bright eyes, and sarcastic wit." She sighs. "I never had a chance not to fall in love with you."

"You loved me then?"

"The way a kid loves anything that's too big for them to fully see. I had no idea about the Acquisition or any of it. You seemed like a cute teenage boy, and I wanted you to think I was cute, too."

"What did I say when we talked?"

She nibbles her bottom lip. "I was sitting at the dining room table, waiting for my mother to finish talking with your mother in her office. You came swaggering in and plopped down in the chair across from me. I tried not to look at you, but you just kept staring at me, so I finally met your eyes. You asked me who I was and what I was doing there. I told you, and then my stomach rumbled really loud. I wanted to crawl under the table and die right there, but you got up and came around to me. You said, 'C'mon.' And you held out your hand.

"I took it, and you led me into the kitchen and

pulled down a box of cookies from a high shelf in the pantry.

"'Have as many as you want.' You scooped up a few, winked at me, then left. My mother never let me have sweets. It's like you knew there was a rule you could break, so you went for it."

"Did you eat the cookies?"

"I ate so many I got a stomachache, but I didn't regret it one bit."

"Just being near me had you breaking bad. I love it." I lean close, my lips grazing against hers.

"Lucius." Stella's voice is harsh. "I didn't realize you were bringing a date."

Evie turns to her. "Hi, Stella."

"Hello." Stella doesn't offer her hand, and she certainly doesn't invite us in. Instead, she blocks the door and sizes up Evie with a hawk-like gaze.

"I don't know if you remember me—"

"I remember you just fine." Stella finally looks at me. "You should've warned us."

"Evie's not a threat." I thread her fingers through mine. "We're together."

"Mmm." Stella doesn't seem the least bit convinced.

To her credit, Evie stands patiently as Stella gives her another once-over.

More silence passes, and for a moment I think Stella isn't going to let us in, but then she steps back. "You can have dinner with us, but I'll go ahead and warn you, Evie. If you try anything. *Anything*. I'll put you down. This is my family, my life, and I won't lose them."

Teddy peeks out from behind Stella, his big eyes focused on Evie.

"I'm not here to hurt anyone." Evie gives Teddy a small smile. "And yes, I shot your uncle. But that's before I got to know him. Now I just want to strangle him sometimes."

Teddy smiles. "Daddy says that too."

Stella considers Evie for a few moments longer, then turns and strides away. "The food's almost ready. You two come on in."

"Do you want to see my room?" Teddy asks Evie.

"I don't know if that's a good idea. Your mom might not like it."

"She knows I can take care of myself." Teddy takes Evie's hand. "I killed like ten guys yesterday with a crossbow."

"What?" Evie frowns.

"Target practice. You know. I'm getting better. Mom says so, and she's the best shot ever."

"I have no doubt of that. She means business."

"Come on. I promise I won't shoot you." Teddy pulls on her hand.

"Go ahead. Just don't let him steal you from me." I kiss her neck and release her other hand.

"Teddy, go easy."

"Okay." He grins and pulls her over to the stairs.

As she climbs behind him, she gives me a worried look.

I blow her a kiss and stride down to the kitchen.

Sin and Stella are inside, both deep in conversation. Sin has a swollen cheek and a black eye from our run-in yesterday.

"Yikes, you look like shit." I lean against the pantry door.

"Lift up your shirt." He points at my side.

"I beg your pardon. I'm a *gentleman*."

"You've never been a gentleman a day in your life." Stella angrily yanks a pan of baby potatoes from the oven.

"Those smell amazing."

"Rosemary and garlic." She slams the pan on the trivet and whirls on me. "What the hell are you thinking bringing her here?" She leans over to look past me. "And where the fuck is she?"

"Teddy dragged her to his lair."

Stella's eyes widen. "You let her go with—"

"Teddy will be fine. Besides, if anything happens, his scream is supersonic." I hold my hands up. "Just trust me, okay?"

Sin glowers. "I'll go check on them." He lumbers off, his resting bitch face doing double time with all those bruises.

Stella walks to the ovens and stares at whatever is cooking in the top one. "I haven't seen her since that night. She looks ... different."

"Blonde hair is weird on her, right?"

"Not just that." She puts her hands on her hips, her black tank top and workout pants making her look like an angry assassin. "She's been through shit. Not like me. Not that horrible." She hangs her head. "But I can tell what happened changed her."

"She's strong now."

Stella turns, her green eyes looking tired. "What are you doing, Lucius? Since when have you wanted just one woman? Since when have you actually thought about a real future?"

"I guess taking a slug to the chest makes you reconsider things." I reach over and grab one of the hot potato halves and toss it into my mouth. "There's just something about her. It was instant. Even before I spoke to her, when I only knew her as a ghost at the edge of my property. It's like we're linked. I can't describe it. I really wish I could."

"You sure you aren't just turned on by the idea of her killing you or some twisted crap like that?" She rubs her temples and closes her eyes. "Because that's you to a 't'—just looking for some sort of bizarre thrill."

"It's not like that, though, I mean yeah. That'll be a great story to tell our grandchildren one day."

Her eyes pop open. "What. The. Fuck? Did you just say grandchildren? You've *never* talked about wanting kids. Not one damn day of your life! What the hell has she done to you? Are you drugged or something?" She steps closer and peers up at me.

"In a way, yes. I'm in love."

She stands for a moment, her eyes searching my face. But I've laid my cards on the table, and there's nothing I can do to change them. Evie has gotten to me in a way no one ever has, and I know that no one else ever will.

"Holy shit." She backs up and sits on a stool by the island. "You're serious."

"Very."

"Does she love you?" she asks.

"She said 'I think I love you' and I'm sort of going on faith that it will eventually turn into a full 'I love you' replete with adoration and blowjobs."

"God, she doesn't even know what she's getting herself into. Your drinking, your sarcasm, your fatalism." She stops rubbing her temples and sits up. "Someone should warn her."

"She's been stalking me for weeks, months even. I think she knows about all those things."

She holds up a finger. "Okay, so how do you know she isn't just playing you? Hmm?"

"I know you're deprived because you married my brother, but trust me, Stella, when you give a woman as many orgasms as I've already given Evie, you can taste the truth on her."

"Gross." She stands right as the oven starts beeping. "I hope you're right. I really do. Because if you're not ..."

"I trust her. Would I have let her go play with Teddy if I had any doubt about her?"

Stella sighs and pulls out the hot roast. "No."

"Okay. Trust me about her."

"I'll try. But if she tries to hurt any of us—including you—" She rams a thermometer into the meat.

"Point taken."

"Good." She peers at the reading, then pulls the thermometer out, seemingly satisfied. "What about this guy that killed the Sovereign? Sin told me he has a thing for Evie?"

"He's gone silent. I've had my contacts looking for him everywhere, but he's disappeared. I guess after the bloodbath he pulled at the party, he's come to his senses and realized killing the Sovereign wasn't a great idea. The rest of them are probably after his head, if they haven't got it already."

"If he's busy avoiding them, that's one less thing we have to worry about, so I'm all for it." She pulls out a long knife to slice the roast. "But if he's as much of a loose cannon as he seems, he's far more dangerous than the rest of them. They go by their 'rules' to a fault, including the 'untouchable Sovereign' one. It's the only reason they haven't started a full-on war with us. If this Charles doesn't care about the rules, then he's a completely different animal."

She's right about that.

"We'll find him. I've already had my people check in at Beau Corrigan's. His widow is still there; otherwise, the place is empty. We've checked all his homes—asshole has a plum condo in the Warehouse district—he hasn't been back. I've put lookouts all over the place for him." I want to catch him quickly and put him down like the rabid dog he is. If he bit the hand of his master so easily, he'll have no problems coming after Evie.

"If he comes for us, he's mine." She slices through the meat with finesse.

"If he comes here, he's even dumber than I thought." I can't imagine the fun Sin and Stella would have carving up that raging dickhead.

I turn when I hear footsteps on the front stairs, then walk out to meet Teddy, Sin, and Evie.

"Everything all right?" I ask her.

"I showed her my Lego Hogwarts." Teddy is beaming up at her. "She loved it."

"He's Slytherin." She raises her eyebrows.

"It's the best house, don't you think?" He walks into the dining room with her as Sin shoots me a dark look.

"What? Has she done anything wrong at all?"

"No, but—"

"Give her a chance." I put my hand on his shoulder and keep him in the hall as Teddy regales Evie with all the reasons why Slytherin is the best house. "I know I've made so many fucking mistakes, but she's not one of them. Can you please trust me on this?"

"Has she returned the iPad?" he asks sharply.

"No, but she will once she feels safe."

"She doesn't feel safe with you?"

"No, she doesn't feel safe with *you*. She's worried that if she turns it over, you might go after her... Not that I'd let you hurt her."

He considers me for a while, then asks, "When you aren't with her, are you thinking about her?"

"Yes."

"Is she the first thing you think about when you wake up and the last thing before you fall asleep? Can you handle her quirks, however odd they may be? Do you want to hurt her? To make her cry? To put her back together? To lift her up? To please her even when what she needs might hurt you? Can you give her what she needs in bed, and can she give you what you need? And, most of all, can you two be together even though you killed Red?"

"What are you, a couples therapist?"

"I'm serious, Lucius. I've been married for long enough to know that these are the things that matter."

"Yes to all of those questions and more. I don't know how to convince you of what I feel in here." I tap my sore chest. "But it's real."

He wrinkles his nose at the thought of me having a heart, then glances into the dining room. "Look, I know you're a foolhardy dumbass who makes split-second decisions without enough information. But this is so far out of your usual MO that I'm somewhat curious to see how it ends. Then again, Stella and I are together despite all of our ... *history*. So maybe this makes more sense than it should."

That's as close to 'I'll give her a chance' as I'm going to get out of Sin.

"That smells amazing." Evie leans over as Stella places the roast on the table. "Can I help you with anything in the kitchen? I'm happy to—"

"When are they going to be potty trained?" Teddy hustles in with Renee tucked under one arm and Rebecca under the other. "They just crop dusted me, then finished the job with a sprinkling of poop napalm. I almost vomited, and this is *after* my rotation in the ER." He pauses when he spots Evie, then recovers quickly and hands Renee to Stella.

"They don't smell that bad." Stella takes Renee and kisses her nose before sliding her into her highchair. "They're just well-seasoned."

"You're fooling yourself. It's toxic waste." Teddy puts Rebecca in her matching high chair, then turns to Evie. "I didn't know you'd be here tonight, but I'm happy to see you and everyone getting along so well." He gives her his Teddy smile, so genuine that I want to backhand him sometimes.

"Thank you. I know it's weird—"

"Understatement," Stella mutters as she heads back to the kitchen with Sin at her heels.

"But I'm just glad to be included," Evie finishes.

"Stella's a great cook. You're going to love this." He

sits across from her and little Teddy as I pour drinks for everyone. I sneak a shot of bourbon, but then I catch Evie watching me out of the corner of her eye.

Without missing a beat, she says, "I know how to cook, but really only for one. I wouldn't know where to start with making a meal this big."

"I'm going to learn to cook," little Teddy announces while staring up at Evie with what can only be described as heart eyes. "Whatever your favorite food is, I'm going to cook it."

Big Teddy and I exchange an amused look.

"Easy there, tiger." Teddy serves up a plate for him as I start cutting the twins' food into tiny pieces. "I think Uncle Lucius already staked his claim."

"Doesn't mean anything." Undeterred, my nephew keeps staring in adoration. "What's your favorite food? I bet Uncle Lucius doesn't even know."

"Well, hmm."

"I know what she really seems to enjoy. Tube steak." I waggle my brows at her.

Teddy almost chokes on his ice water.

"Tube steak? I can make that. Easy." Little Teddy gives me a challenging stare.

"No, but thank you for that, Lucius." Evie shakes her head and somehow keeps a straight face. "It's homemade macaroni and cheese, especially if it has bacon in it."

"Mommy can teach me, and the next time you come over, I'll make some for you." He forks a piece of pork tenderloin and plops it into his mouth with pure satisfaction.

What am I going to do with this kid?

I scoop some mashed potatoes out for Renee and Rebecca who babble at me. Renee immediately grabs the potatoes with her meaty paw and smears some on my shoulder.

Evie watches, surprise twinkling in her eyes. "You really are all close, aren't you?"

"We are, well, at least until Sin and Lucius get into a tussle, throw themselves out a window, and continue fighting on the lawn." Teddy points his fork at me. "I still think you should get imaging of your ribs."

"No thanks, Doc McStuffins." I serve the twins who discuss the food options among themselves in cute baby babble.

Teddy sighs. "Never change, Lucius, you miserable jerk." He can't hide his smile at the end. He really is the nicest Vinemont. Freak.

Evie looks around for a while, then pushes back her chair and stands. "I'm sorry. Excuse me for a moment." She walks out, and little Teddy stands to follow her.

"This one's all mine. Sorry, buddy." I tousle his hair and follow Evie down the hall to the powder room.

Sin and Stella pass me with questioning glances, but I just wave them to the dining room.

Standing right at the powder room door, I knock softly. "Evie, you okay?"

"I'm fine. Please go be with your family."

"What's wrong?"

"Nothing."

"I can tell it's something. Can I come in?" I can hear her sniffle, and a few moments later she opens the door a crack.

I push it all the way open and shut it behind me. "What's wrong?" I cup her face with my hands and wipe her tears away with my thumbs.

"Nothing. Everything. I don't know." She sniffles again, and I pull her into my arms.

"Are you worried about Stella?" I kiss her hair. "She hasn't thrown a knife at you yet. That's a win as far as I'm concerned. I think it'll just take some time for her to really warm up."

"No. She's actually been fine." She takes a deep, shuddering breath and lets it out. "It's just, I never had that. A family. Not really. My mom raised me to marry me off to someone in the society. My dad—I barely even saw him. He was always at the office, or playing golf, or doing anything other than being around his children. Most of the time, I was alone. The only one I ever had was …"

"Red." I sigh. "I'm sorry, Evie."

"You said you'd never apologize." She looks up at me, her eyes wet with tears.

"I'll do whatever you want as long as you stop crying." I wipe her cheeks again.

"I don't know. It just sort of hit me when I saw how

tightknit all of you are. No wonder Sin was so angry at you for being with me. He's scared for his family." She laughs a little. "I never expected Sinclair Vinemont to be afraid of *anything*. But he is, because he loves everyone in this house, including you."

"Oh, darlin'." I kiss her forehead. "How many times do I have to tell you that I am *extremely* lovable?"

She laughs again, and I realize I love the sound of it. I'm a complete sap for this woman. Sin was right.

"Now, can we get back to dinner? If we don't eat, Stella might demonstrate her crossbow mastery on us."

"One more thing." She gestures toward the door.

"What's that?" I follow her out, down the hall, and out to the car.

She reaches behind her seat and pulls out the damaged iPad. "Here."

I try not to crow about winning her trust. "I didn't realize it was so bad off. I don't even know if my computer guys can save it." I take it from her. "You were planning this all along?"

"I decided I want your family to trust me more than I want an insurance policy, and I want to find the people who are trying to destroy all of us."

"If we can get that list, we'll take their legs out from under them." I walk her up the steps. The front curtains twitch, and I'm certain Sin and Stella just saw what happened.

"I'm scared." She shakes out her hands. "What if they all still hate me?"

"Sin's hated me for years, but he still keeps me around." I lean close to her ear. "It's because he's jealous of my good looks and big—"

She smacks my chest and laughs. "You aren't fooling me at all. Even though you two fight hard, you love harder."

"It's a good thing I love you, then." I kiss her forehead.

She looks up at me. "I'm not alone anymore, am I?" she whispers.

"Never again." I kiss her, sealing that promise with all my heart.

29

EVIE

*L*inton rubs his eyes. "Two weeks ago, we were going to pare Magnolia down to its basic building blocks with a hostile takeover, one that would make the Vinemonts our enemies for life. But, let me get this straight, now we're going to work *with* the Vinemonts?"

"Yes."

"Do you have any idea how hard it was for me to reconvene the board?"

"Yes." I flip through the prospectus I've been working on for days and nights on end. It's an even more comprehensive vision for Magnolia than my original sales pitch.

"Will you tell me what's going on?" He sounds tired. "What part of your plan is this? You're playing them, I get it. But what's the endgame?"

"I'm not playing anyone. This plan—" I tap the

prospectus. "Is going to put Magnolia Sugar back on top. From supplying large hotel chains and restaurants all the way to bags of sugar sitting on store shelves, we can streamline this company and get so much more from the market."

"I'm lost."

"I'm not trying to ruin anyone." I finally look at him. "Not anymore."

"First you dye your hair red—"

"It's my natural color."

"Okay, well, it's a change. Then you change this. I'm just trying to figure out what's going on. Why the sudden flip?"

Lucius, Sin, and Stella walk into the office, each of them striking in their own way. Stella's hair is red like mine, but also not like mine at all. I'm a strawberry blonde, but she's got dark red locks and bright green eyes. Beautiful and fierce. Sin is the same tall, glowering wall I've always known. And Lucius—he makes my knees go weak when he turns to give me his signature half smile. No wonder my teen self was beyond obsessed with him. My adult self is, too.

"Hi." I greet him as he walks through the door of the board room.

"Darling, you look utterly fuckable." Lucius comes over and kisses me. He doesn't care if the whole staff of Magnolia's corporate office sees.

Linton clears his throat.

"Problem?" Sin asks.

Linton stutters out a 'no.'

When Lucius finally pulls back, he stares down at me. "Ready?"

"Yes."

Stella walks to my other side and peers down at the prospectus. "You're certain this is what's best for Magnolia?"

"I know some of the ideas in here might seem a little harsh or outlandish, but I promise you this is my best work. I've taken other companies far on their journeys toward large profit margins, but Magnolia is going to be the best one yet."

Stella turns to me. "If you can convince the board and Sin—" She shoots Lucius a wry look. "You've already got this one in your pocket. I'm filling in for Teddy, so you'll have to convince me as well."

"I know, and I ..." I meet her gaze. "I have a lot to make up for. For me ..." God, this is so hard. "And for my brother."

She blinks as if I'd slapped her.

Lucius and Sin share a look and leave the room, followed by an openly confused Linton.

"What your brother did isn't your fault." She says it through tight lips.

"I know, but I also know that the things he did to you, well, I'll never be able to understand it all. I just want you to know that I know he was vicious and cruel to you. And I'm sorry, even if I'm not to blame for it."

She stays silent for long moments that seem to

stretch on at an agonizingly slow pace. "Red was a horrible person," she says carefully. "There's no doubt about that in my mind. But I have experience there. My father—he was horrible, too. I saw it, but I refused to believe it until the Acquisition. Then I couldn't deny it any longer. I loved him anyway. Despite everything he'd done, I think he cared about me in that horrible, self-aggrandizing way that narcissists do." She keeps peering at me, her gaze searching mine. "I understand the conflict in you. And Lucius trusts you. He and I have had our differences—*plenty* of them—but if he has faith in you, then I'm willing to give you a chance. A real one." She nods, as if to herself. "Do you know how to shoot?"

"I'm not too bad, as long as the target is pretty close."

Her lips turn up in a devious smile. "Well, yes I suppose you can. Lucius is a testament to it. So, can you fight?"

"A little. I took self-defense courses, but I've learned I need work."

She finally smiles, and I realize she's being honest with me—she really is going to give me a chance. "All right. Once we're done with the show here and you're rolling on the restructure—if that's what we choose—I'm going to start your bootcamp."

"Coming from you, that sounds terrifying," I admit.

She laughs. "I promise, when I first met Sin and

Lucius, I was soft. Like a cute little kitten with no idea how to run with the wolves."

I vaguely know her history from catching snippets here and there from Red, but I'm still impressed by her. She's overcome everything to be who she is.

"Next Saturday. Six o'clock. I want you at my place ready to work." She sticks her hand out, the vining tattoos crossing the back of her hand and circling her ring finger.

"I'm scared but also excited." I shake, her grip firm.

"Perfect." She smiles and strides out to have a word with Sin in the hall. Lucius is waiting at the door to the boardroom, his eyes on me.

I take my box of papers and meet him there.

"How'd it go?"

"She wants to train me."

He groans. "Fuck, you're going to be even hotter if you know how to drop me."

"I like the thought of that." I sweep past him and greet the board. This time, I'm not alone. And this time, I won't fail.

~

I WAKE UP WITH A START, then realize Lucius has slid on top of me, his hard body pressing me down into the bed.

"Good morning," he murmurs against my neck.

"It certainly is." I run my hands down his back and just enjoy his kisses. Then I jolt.

"What?" He meets my gaze.

"I have to meet Stella. I won't be late." I push against him, but he doesn't move.

"We've been working all week. Are you sure you have to go right now?"

I twist to see the clock on the nightstand. "Oh my god, I don't even have time to shower!"

"What's a few minutes between new friends?" He runs his tongue down my chest, his cock already nudging at my entrance.

"I'm going to get there on time and make a good impression or so help me, Lucius, I'll come back here and shoot you again."

"Well, when you put it like that..." He groans and rolls away from me.

I jump up and run to the bathroom, finding my toothbrush and going to work on my teeth with one hand as I dig around in the pile of clean clothes I'd brought with me to Lucius's house.

He stands in the doorway watching me, his nude form so damn delectable in the morning light.

"Stop trying to tempt me." I spit, then grab an elastic and whip my hair into a ponytail.

He scrubs a hand down his face as he stares at my ass. "You know, I set the alarm clock forward fifteen minutes."

I rinse the toothpaste out of my mouth. "What?"

"I set the clock ahead so you wouldn't be late. I know how much this means to you."

Turning, I ask, "Are you being serious?"

"Yes. Why would I lie about getting up even earlier?" He scratches his head.

His cock is at full attention.

I saunter toward him, and his eyes light with heat. "So I have time?"

"Yes." He nods, then reaches out and pulls me to him. "Time for some quick stress relief." He lifts me by my ass, and I squeal as he carries me to the bed.

"Put me down." I bite his shoulder.

"Only if it's on my cock." He kneads my ass.

"No. You sit." I point to the bed.

"Oh." He puts me down. "I see."

"Not yet, but you will." I drop to my knees in front of him.

He doesn't sit, just stares down at me as he fists his thick cock. "You going to suck me like a good girl?" His husky tone makes my core hot and wet.

I open my mouth, waiting.

He groans at the sight and presses his head against my tongue. "I'm going to paint this white, Evie. You want that?"

In answer, I take him to the back of my throat.

His hips jerk forward, and he grips my ponytail with one hand. I dig my nails into the backs of his thighs, my body on fire for him as I start nodding on his cock. He's thick and so, so hard. A little drool slips from my lips, and I try to back off to wipe it away, but he holds onto my ponytail, guiding me forward. I swallow, my throat contracting around his head.

He groans and stares down at me. "Such a good fucking girl."

I slip one hand between my legs as I work my tongue along his shaft.

"Fuck yes, play with that pussy." He tightens his grip on my ponytail and thrusts into my mouth. He's pure dominance, taking what he wants as I stroke my clit and hollow my cheeks.

My tension mounts, my body singing with arousal as I roll my hips against my fingers.

"Ah fuck." He thrusts harder.

I gag a little, my eyes watering, and the next time he meets my gaze, he looks almost unhinged. So damn sexy, so caught up in the two of us.

"I'm going to come on that pink tongue," he grates. "Show it to me." He grabs my other hand and wraps it around his cock.

I open my mouth and stick out my tongue. Somehow, the utter filthiness of it turns me on even more. My orgasm hits from everywhere all at once. I moan as I come, my pussy throbbing with each wave of pleasure.

Lucius grunts, his cock thickening even more, and then he sprays my tongue, coating it with him as I lick his head and get as much of him as I can. When he's spent, I close my mouth and swallow.

He staggers back and sits on the bed. "Holy shit." He looks at me, at the come dripping along my chin. "You're like the Sistine Chapel. Just look at that art."

I roll my eyes. "Ridiculous."

"I don't know if I can just let you leave here after that. I mean, what if you change your mind about me while you're gone? Then what, Evie? I'll never get head this epic again? I can't let that happen." He reaches out and pulls me to my feet.

"I suppose you should take good care of me while I'm here and hope for the best while I'm not." I follow him to the bathroom where he wets a washcloth and brings it to my face. "I hate to do this, but I suppose I must." He sighs as he cleans me up. "All gone." He kisses me.

I glance past him at the clock. "Shit." I whirl and start throwing on my clothes. "I've got to go."

"Just promise me you'll come back."

"You're that worried about losing epic head?" I laugh and grab my car keys as I sprint toward the stairs.

"I'm worried about losing you." He follows me.

"Not happening." I run back to him, kiss him again, then dash down the stairs.

When I drive away, he's standing in the broken window—now covered with clear plastic—still naked. How can one man be so aggressive and yet so sweet at the same time? I'll never know.

I reach the end of his drive and turn right, the sun

still low on the horizon. My foot pushes on the gas a little much, but I refuse to be late.

Trees whoosh by, and I'm making good time.

Until a black car shoots out into the road right in front of me.

I hit it broadside. I close my eyes at impact, and the last thing I hear is the sound of a horn blaring.

30

LUCIUS

I hop in the shower, then get dressed. Time ticks by slowly as I wonder how Evie is doing at Stella's bootcamp. I hope Evie doesn't come back too banged up. Then again, Stella knows what it takes to survive. Evie can only benefit from her knowledge. Something niggles at the back of my mind. Worry. But I have to let it go.

Pouring myself a coffee, I eye my liquor cabinet. There have been plenty of mornings where I add a little kick to my caffeine. I'm tempted to do it right now. But I already told Evie I'm trying to be a better man for her.

I stare a little while longer, then sip my coffee. "Okay, fine. I'll be a fine, upstanding gent who doesn't drink until lunchtime." I toast my reflection in the mirrored bar cabinet and take a bigger gulp. It burns. Like alcohol. Good. I'll just pretend it is.

After checking my emails and doing some work—mostly signing contracts and checking in with the sugar farms—I leave off and glance out the window, hoping to see Evie coming home. *Home.* I'm already thinking of this place as our home. I wonder if she thinks of it that way too? Or will she want to leave again? I wouldn't blame her, but my roots are here, just like hers. We'll work it out.

I flip over to my high security server and check my other emails. One of my contacts has been working on repairing and then breaking into the iPad but has had zero luck so far. She's sent me an update of "still can't fucking get this thing working." I'm growing tired of waiting, but I have time. I'll wait as long as I have to in order to find all those assholes and wipe them out.

I finish my coffee and check the clock. It's almost ten in the morning. Shouldn't she be finished by now? Stella must really be working her over. Maybe I should head over there, make sure Evie isn't maimed or anything too serious.

Grabbing my keys, I head down and start up the Lambo. It purrs so beautifully for me. I might name it Evie. The sun is already getting up high in the sky, the humid day cloudless and sticky.

When I turn toward Sin's house, the niggling sensation returns. I don't know why, but I speed even faster down the back road, sending up dust as my tires prowl across the tired pavement.

A few miles from my place, I see some marks in the

road. They're new. I pull up beside the spot and get out. Tire marks, radiator fluid, oil, and gasoline. Bits of metal and fiberglass litter the roadside, but there aren't any cars.

That niggling in the back of my mind turns into full-blown fear. I get back into the car and dial Stella.

She picks up on the second ring. "If you're calling to apologize for your new girlfriend ghosting on me this morning, I don't accept. I got up at the—"

"Evie never showed?"

There must be something in my voice, because Stella stows her sassy tone. "No. What's wrong?"

"She left hours ago. Coming straight to your place. She was so worried she'd be late, and she didn't want to disappoint you. She has to be there." My knuckles are white on the steering wheel, and my stomach is churning.

"She's not. Shit." She muffles the receiver and yells, "Sin!"

I can hear him in the background.

"She left Lucius's place hours ago, but she never showed."

"I just found a place on the road a few miles from my house. There had been a car wreck, but the entire thing was cleared when I got there. No one around."

"Ambush, has to be," Sin says.

"That Charles motherfucker. He's the only one crazy enough to come onto our fucking turf and do something this dumb." I toss the phone, yanking the parking brake, and whip my wheel hard to the left. The tires screech as I turn a 180, then shoot back down the road toward my place.

I grab the phone again.

"—iPad is the only way we're going to find him," Sin says.

"The iPad, sure. But I know where that fucker Corrigan lived. He has to have more family there somewhere."

"You're going back to that house?"

"First, I'm going to my house and getting firepower, then I'm going to the city."

"Lucius, you shouldn't go it alone."

"I'm not waiting. Not when Evie's been fucking *stolen*. You didn't see this guy, Sin. He's a sick bastard. He'll hurt her in ways she won't be able to come back from."

"I'll meet you there," he says.

"No. Protect the family. If he did something this brazen, there's no telling what he'll do next. You have to keep everyone safe. Call Teddy. Put him on alert." I end the call.

The phone rings as I tear down my driveway. It's Sin.

I ignore it and turn the ringer off.

My focus is on Evie.

I will find her, and then I will kill the motherfucker who took her in the most painful way possible.

31

EVIE

My head throbs, and my right arm aches as consciousness hits me like a fiery whip. I'm sore all over, but I can't remember why.

When I open my eyes, I realize I'm in a strange bed in a strange room. I try to sit up, but my head swims, and my arm feels like it's disjointed. Something's wrong with it. Something bad. Nausea rises in my gut, my mouth watering.

I close my eyes and try to breathe slowly. Calm. I have to stay calm.

A horn blares, and I jump. But when I open my eyes again, I'm in the same room. No car. No horn.

A black sedan pops into my vision. That's it. That's what happened. A car wreck. Shit. But where am I? Is this some sort of swank hospital? I don't think so, especially since I'm not getting any treatment.

"Hello?" I call.

Nothing happens.

I try to sit up again, and though the world swims, I force myself to stay upright. Something tickles at my lip, and I reach up to find dried blood there. I must've busted my nose in the accident. God, I hope no one else got hurt.

The room comes into clearer focus now. Brocade wallpaper, Mediterranean accents, lots of gold. Definitely not a hospital.

"Hello?" I call again. I want to get up, to try and find my phone or a way out, but my head pounds in a way that promises a nasty fall if I move too fast.

A sound behind me catches my attention, and I turn. Too fast. The nausea rises again as the pain in my head explodes. I bend over and dry heave.

"Sorry." A woman comes around the bed, her clothes wrinkled, both of her eyes black. "He'll be back soon. I'm supposed to check on you."

"Who?"

"What do you mean?" She wrings her hands.

"Who'll be back soon?"

"My nephew, of course." She glances around, every movement of hers nervous or scared. "The Sovereign."

"What?" I'm lost in this conversation, but I realize I'm in danger. Any talk of Sovereigns means my life is on the line. I have to get out of here. "I need to go." I try to stand, but my vision starts going dark at the edges, so I sit back down. My right arm is limp, my fingers not obeying my commands. I think it might be broken.

"Stay put. He doesn't want you to move too much." She stares down at me, something in her eyes akin to pity. "If you don't obey him, he'll hurt you. And you already have a concussion. And your arm ..." She reaches for it, but I recoil.

"Where's my phone?"

She shakes her head sadly. "No phones. No way out. I learned that the hard way." She points to her bruised face. "Don't make my mistakes. Respect him. He's the authority. The true Sovereign. I only wish I'd seen it earlier."

"We need to leave. We have to go right now."

"And defy the Sovereign? No."

"Sinclair Vinemont is the Sovereign."

She slaps me so hard and so quickly I don't even feel my body hit the floor. I'm speaking to her one moment, and the next I'm in a heap on the rug. I think I'm going to die right here, right now. My head feels like it's splitting open, and I can barely breathe through the pain.

"Look what you made me do. You shouldn't tell lies like that."

I close my eyes tightly and try to block out the agony in my head. But I feel her pulling me up and placing me back on the bed. She's crazy. Whatever Charles has done to her has driven her over the edge.

"The Vinemonts are filthy traitors. They're the reason my Beau is dead. They're the—"

"Charles killed Beau." My voice works, but it sounds like it's coming through a tunnel.

"Lucius Vinemont killed Beau. Charles told me."

"Charles killed him. Slit his throat. I saw the whole thing."

"It doesn't matter. None of it matters. Don't you get that? Charles is the Sovereign now. It's ordained by all those who came before us. Charles is the pinnacle of the Acquisition."

Charles. It all clicks now. This must be a room in that Garden District mansion where the party was held. This woman is Beau's widow, and Charles has taken over everything. It's so much worse than we thought. Charles has been hiding in plain sight. "He can't be the Sovereign. The rules—"

"He doesn't *care* about the rules, you foolish girl. Don't you get it? His word is law. He'll kill anyone who stands against him. He is the Sovereign, and not for ten years. He will reign as Sovereign for as long as he lives," she hisses next to my ear. "Don't say otherwise. I've already warned you."

"Why am I here?" I swallow, my dry throat feeling like shards of glass.

"He wants a pure line. He wants his firstborn son to inherit his mantle."

I'm in so much pain, but just the thought of Charles touching me makes me dry heave again.

Everything hurts, and I want to scream. But no one will hear me. Lucius probably hasn't realized I'm gone. I'm trapped.

Tears roll from the corners of my eyes as my door closes. I don't look, but I can feel the woman left and the room is now empty except for me. Taking deep breaths, I wrestle my emotions into check. I have to be cool and calculating if I want to make it out of here. And I will—because I will never go along with this. But Charles isn't the type to care if I agree or not. He'll hurt me, and there's no one to stop him this time.

I force my eyes open again. A scream sticks in my throat as I find Charles staring down at me, a smug smile on his vile face.

"Even like this, you're a beautiful bride."

"I'm not a bride."

"Of course you are." He lets his gaze travel down the length of my body, making me acutely aware of the fact I'm only wearing a sports bra and tight-fitting shorts.

"I'll never marry you."

"You will." He reaches out and strokes the back of his fingers down my cheek.

"Don't touch me." I try to swat his hand away, but he pins my left wrist next to my head.

"You don't seem to understand, Evie. You're mine. To touch as I please." He reaches for my right arm and takes hold of it near the elbow.

"Don't—" I scream when he squeezes it, the pain like a bomb tearing through my body.

"See?" He grins. "Mine." He moves his hand to my chest and flattens his palm there. "Your heart is beating so fast. I think it's love." He slides it lower and cups my breast.

Tears burn in my eyes. I can't stop him, can't do anything except endure it.

"You don't have to like me, Evie. You just have to take my cock whenever I want to fuck you. I want to make heirs. Plenty of them. You're going to do that for me. Our bloodline will be the heart of the new Acquisition."

"They'll never accept you." I sneer at him. "You killed Beau. You fucked up their entire rulebook."

"Rules." He tsks and moves his hand to my stomach. "That's why the Vinemonts were able to wreck the whole thing. Everyone was too concerned with following the rules, and not concerned enough with the threat they were facing. That won't happen to me. The rules are mine to write now. You'll see."

"It won't work."

"It will. But you don't have to worry yourself with any of that. Just do what I tell you, open your legs when I say, and give me what I want. It's so simple, really. My aunt can't seem to follow those instructions, but I'm sure you can. What, with all your career-girl bullshit."

"I will never give you what you want." I spit in his

face, the final shard of my courage in that one movement.

He wipes his face clean and leans down to me. "You don't have to give it to me, Evie. I'm going to take what I want as many times as I want. Being Lucius's whore is nothing compared to what I'm going to do to you." He licks my chest, his tongue hot and slimy.

"Get off me!" I scream.

"I don't think I will." He leers at me and reaches for my shorts. "I think I'll make my first heir right here, right now."

"No!" I scream and struggle, fighting him as best I can.

He grabs my broken arm and twists it.

I scream so loud and hard I taste blood.

"You're going to give me everything, Evie. Starting with your dirty cunt. I know you let Lucius have it. I'm not dumb. But I'm going to split you in two, so you always know I'm the one who owns you."

"Stop!" I press my thighs together as hard as I can as he yanks my shorts down.

"Um, Charles?"

"What?" he barks at the woman from earlier who's appeared in the doorway.

"The motion detectors just went off. Someone's in the garden by the fountain."

"Which one?" he asks.

"My courtyard. The one with the cherubs." She

keeps her eyes on the floor. "You told me to tell you if—"

"Go," he orders.

She disappears as he climbs off me.

"When I get back, you'd better be naked with your legs spread. If you aren't, I'll break your other arm." He stomps out and slams the door.

32

LUCIUS

I have to start somewhere. The Corrigan mansion is dark, none of the bright lights and milling crowd that it was just a few weeks ago. I wonder if they buried poor Beau Corrigan somewhere on the grounds. Likely.

Jumping the fence at the back of the property, I make my way through the fragrant gardens in the fading afternoon light. Evie's been missing for hours. Each moment that ticks by, the more worry eats away at me. This kind of fear isn't something I'm used to. I'm always doing some sort of violent, vicious shit, and I have no qualms about any of it. But now, when it's Evie's life on the line, it's a completely different sensation. It's nothing short of terror.

I crouch low as I enter one of the courtyards with a fountain. There have to be at least half a dozen all around the house. I lean against it and peer up at the house.

My sources said the only one here is Beau's widow. I'm going to find her and get her to tell me where her freak of a nephew is. Time's wasting, but still I wait by the fountain. Something is off. The hair on my arms is standing on end as I try to see through the windows for any sign of life.

I creep forward, around the side of the fountain, and get a better look through the windows. Everything inside is dark and silent, as if this place is a museum that's closed to visitors.

I can't spare another second, so I stand and stride toward the nearest window.

"I was wondering if you'd show up. How'd you find me?"

I whirl and find Charles walking toward me from the rear of the house.

"Where is she?" I pull my pistol and aim it at him. "Let me see your fucking hands."

"She belongs to me now. As Sovereign, I take what I want." He holds his hands up.

"You aren't the Sovereign."

"I'm not?" He smiles. "But seriously, how'd you find me?"

"You're the typical idiot who goes right back to the scene of the crime. It's actually so fucking stupid—*so fucking stupid*—that I didn't even expect you to be here. I gave you too much credit, you hulking buffoon. I was looking for Beau's widow."

"Ah." He frowns. "I see. Well, I suppose that's good luck on my part. Getting rid of you right off the bat will show the others I'm the real deal."

"After what you pulled, they aren't going to back you."

"You sure about that?" He puts one finger down.

I feel the searing pain in my leg before I hear the crack of the gun. "Fuck!" I drop to one knee, my left calf on fire.

He shakes his head. "The famous Lucius Vinemont. Look at you now. Not so tough without your brothers, are you?"

"I'm plenty tough, asshole. Come closer and find out." I keep my gun aimed at him.

"Honestly, I should thank you. Your family broke all the rules. You were the forerunners for me. I did the same and took my place as Sovereign. I have the backing of the most important society members, and the ones who don't want to go along?" He shrugs. "They'll get buried in a mass grave right beside you and your family."

"If you think you have any chance against my family, you're going to be sorely disappointed." I grit my teeth against the pain and get back to my feet.

"I don't think so. It was so easy to get Evie. She's here, you know? Upstairs in a bedroom, waiting for me to put a baby in her."

"Not going to happen." I aim for his face.

Another bullet rips through me, this time through my right arm. I pull the trigger as my aim falters. I drop the gun, then start to reach for my blade with my left hand, but I stop. And wait.

He ducks, then rises again, untouched. "Almost got me that time. But I'm afraid you're done. And I'm wasting time when I could be balls-deep in your slut. Don't worry, I'll marry her, make an honest woman of her. But she'll never leave this house again. You were smart to be with her all these past weeks. I couldn't find a moment to slide in and take her away. Until this morning. Perfect opportunity. And now she's home for good."

"You'll never break her." I'm slowly moving my left hand toward my belt.

"Wrong. I'm about to break her right now. Like I said, she's spread wide, waiting for me to fuck her. She'll be begging me to come on her face before the night is through." He shrugs. "All right, that's enough. It's time for you to go." He pulls a gun from behind him. "Once you're done, I'll fuck Evie, then head out and kill the rest of the Vinemont rats. You know ..." He pauses and waves his gun to the side. "I've been thinking of taking trophies. Ears maybe? The children's will be really cute all strung up on my headboard like a garland on a Christmas tree. Evie will love it."

Blinding, acid wrath boils up inside me. I can't win this. I know that. Not with a sniper in the trees behind me and this fucking Frankenstein dickhead in front. But I'm not going down alone. I'm taking this asshole with me if it's the last thing I do.

"Nothing to say? No sarcastic last words?" He sneers.

"Nothing you'd understand, you goddamn brick."

"I'll give your regards to Evie. I'm sure she'll—"

I lunge right as he tries to give his stupid goodbye taunt.

He fires, the bullet hitting my chest as I stab up as hard as I can with my blade. The blast knocks me back a pace, the bloody knife still in my hand as I fight through the pain and rush him again. I have to stay close or his sniper will tag me, and I have to do as much damage as I can before that happens. I stab and stab, using all my strength to pierce every fucking organ I can find.

He grunts, his body taking the hits as he brings the gun up again. Another slug pounds into my back. His sniper clearly doesn't give a shit about friendly fire, but I have to stop attacking Charles and use my left hand to grab his wrist.

"You're still going to lose." He fires, the sound deafening so close to my ear. Then he fires again and again, trying his damndest to shoot me in the head. I keep the gun aimed just over my shoulder as I push against his beefy arm with all the strength I have. When the action starts to click instead of firing, I let his arm go, then drop to my ass, keeping my back to the fountain.

His sniper can't reach me here, and I'm able to pick up the knife I dropped.

He still stands in front of me, his face dazed as blood soaks his shirt and pants, so I take the opportunity to stab his motherfucking feet like the petty bastard I am.

When he screams, I grin with delight, then move to his shins, slashing them through his pants.

He stumbles backwards and drops, and when he does his intestines play peekaboo through his tattered shirt.

"You're done, dickhead. So fucking done." I laugh as blood runs from his mouth.

"I'm the Sover—" His eyes roll up in his head, and he falls backward, his body thumping onto the stone patio.

"Hey, asshole!" I yell. "If you want to die like your boss, then keep on shooting. My brothers will be here any second, and they'll happily take you out." I sit still and inspect my wounds. The one in my arm stings like a motherfucker, but it's not fatal. The one in my leg, though, it's gushing. I can't even feel anything past my knee. Not fucking good.

I yank my belt off as I hear something in the tree behind me. Stilling, I listen and barely catch retreating footsteps. I can't believe that worked.

Looping my belt around my thigh, I make a tourniquet as best I can, then lean back. The fountain water splashes on me. Irritating. When I look up at the house, I try to figure out which room Evie's in.

"Hate to break it to you, dumbass," I call to the dead motherfucker beside me. "But there's no way Evie was up there waiting for you to dick her. She's probably got the room rigged to murder you the moment you walk in."

He doesn't respond. In the short time I knew him, he never was a good conversationalist. I laugh at my own joke until my eyes close from fatigue.

I force myself to open them. Then I see something, and I realize I'm hallucinating.

"Evie?" I look at her. She's ghostly white with blood on her lip and in her hair. "You okay?"

"Lucius." She drops beside me, her arm hanging oddly at her side.

"Your arm."

"Lucius. Stay with me." She cups my cheek, and she's right in front of me, but I can barely hear her. "Lucius!"

I close my eyes.

She's screaming for help and begging me to look at her.

I try to. I want to make her happy. "*I'd do anything for you*," I try to tell her. But no words come out, and everything turns into deathly stillness.

33

EVIE

"I hear her!" someone yells.

"Here. We're here!" I scream despite the splitting pain in my head. "Help!"

"Evie!" Teddy runs across the lawn to us, then hurdles the hedge around the fountain. "What happened?"

Sin appears through a side gate, a gun in each hand as he scans the gardens.

I focus on Lucius. "Help him!" I cry to Teddy.

He pulls out his phone and dials 911 as he opens a beaten-up leather bag.

I try to listen to him talk, but I can't take my eyes off Lucius. "—two GSW, major blood loss, AB+, heartbeat—" He presses his stethoscope to Lucius's chest. "—is Afib. Shit. We need medics *now!*" He tosses his phone. "Help me lay him down."

I use my good arm and maneuver Lucius gently

down to the ground. I don't like the way his head lolls on his shoulders or the pallor of his skin.

Teddy gives me a glance. "You're in bad shape, too."

"I'm fine. Please, just save him."

"Sin!" he calls.

Sinclair runs up, guns still in each hand.

"Get this shirt and vest off him while I check his leg."

Sin drops to his knees, and with surprising gentleness, he strips off Lucius's shirt and tears away the vest. "Come on, Lucius. Don't be a dick." He presses his ear to his brother's chest. "It's beating."

"Hand me that gauze." Teddy barks.

I lean over to reach for it, but my head goes fuzzy.

"Evie!" Teddy points at me. "Grab her."

Sin catches me before I hit the ground beside Lucius. I can't seem to control my body. It won't follow even the simplest instructions.

"Save him," I try to say. But I can't tell if the words come out.

"She's concussed, and I don't know what else. Fuck!" Teddy's voice goes in and out. "—keep pressure! I need you to—they're coming. I hear sirens—don't move his arm. Shit, we're losing him!" The anguish in Teddy's voice tears a hole in my heart.

I try to sit up, to do anything and everything to help, but I can't. Lucius needs me, and I'm helpless. It's ripping me apart. He came here to save me, walked right into Charles's trap. It was all for *me*. So much pain. For him. For me. For his whole family. When will it be enough? When will we have suffered enough? I turn my head, even though the agony it causes is like a volcano erupting at the back of my cranium. Lucius is pale and lifeless. His body jerks as Teddy performs CPR.

A wail slips from between my lips. "*I need you.*" I cry. "*Please!*"

Lucius doesn't open his eyes.

With what little strength I can manage, I reach out with my hand and take his. His skin is cold and clammy, but I *know* he's alive. He has to be. I won't give up on him. I can't. Even when my eyes close, even when my head feels like it's about to burst, even when I hear Teddy yell, "I can't get a heartbeat!" Even then, I won't give up. I'll never give up on Lucius.

I force my eyes open one more time, and all I can see is Teddy doing chest compressions, trying to force life back into his brother. The cacophony in my head grows louder, and I can't move anymore. I can't do anything. How did we get here? I can't remember. All I know is that Lucius is hurt. He's dying. He's *dying*.

"*Lucius, please.*" I'll happily beg him—the man I thought was the devil. I'll sell Lucius my soul if it makes him breathe again.

But if it doesn't, I won't let him go alone. Not when I finally know what it feels like to be loved, to be part of a family. "*I'll be with you no matter what. We'll go together. You and me. I promise.*" I smile as I see him smirking at me with his usual devilish flare, his eyes so bright and full of mischief. "*Are you ready? I'm ready.*"

No matter what he's done, he's mine. His sins are as much mine as they are his. Because he's part of me. And now I know I love him more than I've ever loved anyone.

34

LUCIUS

"Evie!" I scream into consciousness with her name on my lips.

"He's awake!" Stella jumps to her feet and rushes to my side.

Sin's already there glowering down at me. "It's about fucking time." He crosses his arms over his chest and looks away. Damn, he must've been truly worried. That reaction from him equates to a mental breakdown for a person with actual emotions.

"Where is she?" I peer around the room, my vision a little out of whack but clearing.

"Lucius." Stella uses a calm tone, one that should be reassuring.

It only causes panic to well up in me. "Evie!" I yell. "Evie!"

A nurse walks in, her sneakers squeaking on the tile floor.

"Where's Evie?"

"Excuse me?" She checks the beeping machines at my bedside.

"Evie Witherington! Where is she?"

"I can't give out information on other pati—"

"She's down the hall. Teddy is with her." Stella steps in front of the nurse. "But you can't see her."

"Why not?"

The nurse finishes her check. "I'll let the doctor know you're awake."

"Teddy knows." Sin taps a message on his phone.

"Dr. Vinemont is *not* his doctor."

"Yes, he is." I don't care what bozo they have assigned to me. No one will take better care of me than Teddy. Not to mention he'll have no problems prescribing me the good stuff.

"Thanks for your help." Stella gives her a pleasant smile. "We're good here."

Stella clearly isn't able to be convincingly sweet anymore, because the nurse scowls as she turns and leaves.

"Evie. Tell me." I stare at Stella.

She glances at Sin.

"Take me to her." I start reaching for the IV stuck in my arm. "Or I'll find her myself."

"She's in a coma." Sin says and swipes my hand away from the tubing. "Teddy did chest compressions on you until the ambulance arrived and continued doing them until they got you hooked up to a compression machine. It kept you alive until they were able to do a blood transfusion to stabilize you, then surgery on your leg and arm to stop the bleeds and remove the slug fragments."

I look around. "How long have I been here? What happened to Evie?"

"Three days." Stella sits in the chair at my bedside. "You've been awake a few times, but you were under anesthesia. She had to have surgery, too, and she hasn't woken up. They're keeping her sedated so she can heal."

"Heal what? What's wrong with her?" I feel like screaming.

"She had a bad concussion that had gone untreated. Her brain started to swell, and they had to drill a hole in her skull to relieve the pressure."

I scrub a shaking hand down my face. "Will she live?"

They exchange another glance.

"Will she live?" I yell.

"They don't know." Sin reaches up and unhooks my IV bag from the stand. "Come on. I'll take you to her."

"He's not supposed to be moved," Stella chides.

"If he dies, he dies," Sin deadpans.

"Too soon." Stella sighs and curls into a ball in her chair.

Something tells me they've slept very little over the past three days.

I try to sit up higher in the bed, and pain ricochets

through my body like another bullet. "Jeez." I groan and lie back.

"You're barely out of the woods. Don't get cocky." Sin maneuvers my bed into the hall, and we roll past room after room.

"Is she going to live?" I feel like a stupid child asking that question.

"She's a fighter. She's proven that." He doesn't say any more. He doesn't have to. If it can be survived, then Evie will survive it.

I clench my eyes shut and try to remember what happened. The last thing I recall is her running to me. She was strong enough to run to me. So this induced coma must be precautionary or something. It can't be that bad.

Sin wheels me into a room at the end near the nurse's station. Teddy stands, his face haggard, his baby beard growing out in golden hairs.

"Any change?" Sin asks.

"No." He comes over and helps pull me into the room. "Good to see you awake." He smiles down at me.

"How is she?" I try to crane my neck up to see her. Once again, the pain punches me in the gut.

"Lie still. We'll put you right beside her." Teddy moves the bed around with practiced ease.

When she comes into view, my heart somehow leaps and sinks at the same time. It's her. Her red hair and fair skin, the pink lips I want to kiss even now. But she's pale, her eyes taped shut, and her head wrapped in gauze. Dark half-moons show under each eye, and a drain runs from underneath the back of her head.

"Her brain isn't swelling more. That's good news." Teddy doesn't look me in the eye.

"What did he do to her? How did this happen? She ran to me at that fucking house. She *ran*. I *saw* her."

"She likely suffered the initial concussion from the car wreck. That's what imaging seems to show, anyway. An initial blow."

"Then what?" I wish I could kill Charles all over again. I wish I could make it hurt so bad his goddamn great-great-grandfather would feel it.

Sin clears his throat. "From what I could piece together, she was locked in a bedroom upstairs at the house. She couldn't get the door open, so she tried throwing herself against it. When that didn't work, she went to the window, probably saw what was happening between you and Charles, and then ..."

I blink as my insides twist and shred. "Are you saying she threw herself out of a fucking window for me?"

"She's a keeper," Sin says nonchalantly, confirming it.

I try to reach for her, but then I notice her arm is in a cast. "The fuck?"

"A simple fracture. Also likely from the wreck," Teddy fills in.

"How long until we know if she'll ... wake up?" For

the first time in as long as I can remember, I fight back tears.

"Could be days, could be weeks."

"I won't give up on her." I turn to Teddy. "Promise me you won't give up on her."

"I won't, but Lucius. There might come a time when letting her go would be the best—"

"No." Despite the pain, I reach out and take her hand. "She never gave up on me. I won't do it to her."

"You need rest as much as she does. Two major surgeries, blood loss, and the damage on your back almost impacted your spine."

"I don't care about any of that shit. I just need her to wake up."

Teddy reaches over and squeezes my shoulder lightly. "She knows you're here. It's amazing what people in comas report once they wake. The things they could hear and sense."

"Wake up, Evie. I'm not fucking around." I blink away my tears and focus on her. "Come back to me."

35

EVIE

My mouth is dry. Like, not just dry. It feels like someone filled it full of chalk. Yuck. I need to get some water from the fridge. God, ice water sounds *amazing* right now. I just need to make sure I don't wake Lucius.

There's a beeping noise. It's super annoying. He needs to change the batteries in his smoke alarm.

I open my eyes and try to roll out of bed.

My throat is so sore. Am I sick? My vision is all fuzz. Did I drink last night? I blink and blink until it starts to clear. Someone's in the room with us. I stare straight ahead. Is it Charles? Has he found me?

The beep gets faster and faster. I can't catch my breath. Something's stealing it away from me. I try to scream, but only a strangled sound comes out.

"Evie!" My name comes from somewhere far away, like I'm playing telephone with soup cans and string.

Another person is here, but this time, I know who it is. Lucius. He leans in front of me, his brown hair falling onto his forehead as he looks down at me.

"Hi, darling." He smiles, and I could swear I see tears in his eyes.

The beeping slows down.

"Hey." My voice is more of a croak.

People are moving in the background. They're talking, but I can't hear them. I'm focused on Lucius as my mind starts to go in reverse, putting the whole thing together. I was at that horrible house with Charles. He was going to ... I look at Lucius.

"Shh." He strokes my hair. "You're safe. I swear, Evie. You're safe with me."

I want to say 'I know.' But my throat hurts too much. Then I realize why. There's a tube. It's why my breathing feels strange.

"She's fighting the tube." Teddy comes into view along with another man in a white coat. He's the one I saw when I woke up.

"Let's go." The man motions toward me, and two nurses come over.

Lucius moves out of their way, but he keeps his hold on my hand.

After a few uncomfortable minutes, the tube is out, and I can breathe freely again. The nurse brings a small toothbrush, and I reach for it, but my muscles are weak. Lucius takes it from her, despite her frown, and brushes my teeth for me. It feels wonderful, like scratching an itch.

I spit in a little plastic pan as best I can, and the nurse cleans up after me.

"Thank you." I already feel tired. How is that possible? I just woke up. But when did I get here?

"You okay?" Lucius is right beside me again, one hand on my face, the other gripping my fingers. "Evie?"

"I'm ... confused."

"Totally normal." Teddy sinks into a chair beside the bed. He looks rough. "We can go back through what happened to get it all straight for you."

"Later." Lucius hovers, and he can't seem to look away.

"Wait." I get a flash of memory. Of him, hurt badly. "Are you okay? Oh my god, you almost died! Did you die? Are we dead?"

"No, darling." He kisses the back of my hand. "No. We're alive."

"What happened?"

Lucius glances at Teddy.

Teddy looks at me for a few moments. "Tell her, but if she starts getting upset, you should stop."

"It's going to be a lot."

I realize Lucius looks worn out just as badly as Teddy. His face is almost gaunt.

Worry tries to fire up inside me. "Are you okay?"

He smiles, and it's a beauty. So sincere it makes me warm all the way down to my toes.

He kisses me so softly, so tenderly. "Darling, as long as you're here, I'm golden."

EPILOGUE 1
LUCIUS

The redesign plans rustle as I creep past them and into our bedroom. Evie is snoring lightly, the covers thrown off, her body like an invitation in the moonlight.

I want to stop and appreciate it more, but I need to wash up. Once I'm in the shower, blood sluices down the drain, and I stand under the spray for several minutes until it runs clear.

The shower door opens. "I didn't know you were going hunting tonight." Her soft hands slide down my arms, though she pauses on my right to run her finger pad over my scar.

"Sin got a lead on one of the names from the iPad. We were just going to do recon, but shit went down." I turn to her.

She looks up at me, and I know I'm home. Not

when I drive onto my property or walk through the front door—only when I'm with her.

"Did you get them?"

"We only had to cull one, but he gave us a lot of trouble until it was done." I turn my head to the side and show her where he landed a pretty good blow. "I think he must've been a boxer in his youth."

She gets on her tiptoes and kisses it. "How many more to go?"

"Ten or so. We've weeded out most of them."

"Any word on Beau's wife?" I hate the concern in her voice when she asks about Gloria.

"Still nothing. Gloria's disappeared. Maybe she started a new life somewhere."

"Maybe." She doesn't sound convinced. "She was just so damn ... creepy. So convinced."

"I know." I kiss her forehead and wrap her in my arms.

"I missed you." She sighs and leans against me.

"I missed you, too. How was training with Stella?"

"She kicked my ass, as usual. But she said I'm getting better at moving my feet."

"That's a big improvement."

"Thanks." She laughs. "I think that was a compliment?"

"It was." I run my hands up and down her back.

"The architect came today, too. She said she thinks she can incorporate our changes, and it'll take about six months of construction."

"As long as they don't dig near the back pasture, we're good."

She shakes her head against me. "How did I end up with the most depraved, violent, angry Vinemont on record?"

"Look, darling. I really don't know how many times I'm going to have to tell you this, but I am *extremely* lovable."

She laughs and leans back, inviting a kiss that I'm happy to give. "You're also the sexiest man I've ever met. The sweetest."

"Sweet, hmm?" I back her against the wall, the tiles still cool despite the warm water. "No one ever calls me that except you."

"Because no one ever experiences your sweet side except me." She runs her hands along my chest.

"It's going to stay that way." I lift her.

She spreads her legs for me, and I nudge my way to her entrance.

When I slide inside her, she bites my shoulder.

Fuck, yes. I give it to her slowly, moving inside her, feeling every bit of her as I make love to her. The water runs down my back as I thrust and touch and suck. Her body was made for me, mine for her.

I go deep, kissing her mouth as I grind against her clit, our slick bodies sliding. "Do you have any idea how much I fucking love you?" I kiss her throat, running my tongue along it and swallowing the water.

"Make me come, and then I'll know for sure."

I grin and lean down to claim one of her nipples in my mouth. I suck and nip at it, then reach down between us and finger her clit.

She digs her nails into my shoulder as I work her, my balls drawing up and demanding I release inside her. But I wait. I give it to her just how she needs it, take her higher and higher.

When I bite down on her other nipple, she comes on an erotic moan, her pussy squeezing me tight as I thrust deep.

"That's my good girl." I claim her mouth and groan as I come inside her. Her cunt is still contracting, milking me as I work my hips. "Such a good fucking girl."

Her toes curl, her body so tight, and then she lets out a breath. "Oh my god," she breathes.

"Thank you." I kiss between her breasts, then lick off the water.

She runs her fingers through my wet hair. "Why are you so good at that?"

"I'm good at everything that pertains to you." I kiss her again lazily, our tongues doing a slow dance with each other.

"You really are." She nods, then takes my hand in hers. Her engagement ring is covered in droplets, yet still sparkles even in the low light.

"What are you—" I stop talking when she places my hand on her stomach.

"You're so good at loving me that it looks like we're going to have to have a shotgun wedding."

I stare.

I keep staring.

I stare even more.

Mini explosions fire inside me, most of them in my chest. I can't breathe. Can't form rational thought.

"But I thought you were on birth control?" That's all I can think to say.

She laughs, and it squeezes my half-mast cock teasingly. "I don't know if you remember, but I was in a coma. No meds. And then—" She shrugs. "Then I just didn't start them up again."

"A baby?" My eyes feel like they're watering, but I'm sure it's just water from the shower spray.

"*Our* baby." She squints. "Are you happy?"

"Are you kidding?" I thrust all the way inside her again. "I'm going to be a father. I'm fucking ecstatic!"

She laughs again, sending my cock into full-on fuck mode. I pull out and slide all the way inside her. "A baby?" I kiss her again and again, unable to stop.

She wraps her arms around my neck and holds on tight as I start a slow rhythm, loving her. "I love you, Lucius."

"I love you, and I already love our baby." I kiss her ear. "I hope she's smart like you."

She nibbles my hear. "I hope he's just as lovable as you."

I lean back and thrust deeper, hitting that spot she loves. "Oh darling, I think we both know *no one* is more lovable than me."

EPILOGUE 2
EVIE

"Now I'm wishing I got some watercolor ink done on mine." Stella runs her fingers down the vine tattoo along my spine. "This is so pretty."

"You can always add to yours." I smooth the skirt of my dress for the millionth time. It hasn't had a wrinkle in it at any time.

"No, I think these look perfect on you." She smiles at me in the mirror and picks up the veil beside me. "I hate to hide it under this."

"If you think I shouldn't—"

"Oh, you definitely should." She smiles and affixes it in my hair with a diamond comb. "I've got fifty bucks that says Lucius is going to cry when he lifts it and sees you."

I laugh. "Who'd you bet?"

"Sin." She keeps fussing with it until she's happy. "There."

I peer at myself in the floor-length mirror. My baby bump isn't showing yet, but I still cup the little roundness at my waist.

"I may have already bought about fifty monogrammed things. Just with the 'V' of course, since we don't know what it is yet."

"Fifty?"

She blushes a little. "I may have gotten carried away. It's just so exciting. I didn't think I'd ever get a sister, you know? I'm always stuck with these Vinemont men. Not that I don't love them. I do. But you know how they are."

"Teddy is definitely the most tolerable."

"Yeah, he's named perfectly. A total teddy bear." She wraps her arms around me from behind, hugging me carefully. "This is going to sound weird and probably kind of creepy, but you make me feel a little bit like the old me sometimes. In a good way. I guess I lost a little bit of that after …"

I turn and meet her gaze. "All I can say is thank you. Thank you for welcoming me …" I smile. "Eventually."

"Eventually." She agrees. "I'm just protective."

"Makes sense. You've got a lot to protect."

"Including you." She steps back and looks me up and down. "You look … Breathtaking."

"Thank you." I try not to cry, but I still tear up.

"Not on my watch!" She darts to grab a tissue as I take deep breaths.

Renee and Rebecca babble to each other in the corner by the fan. They are absolutely adorable in their little pink flower girl dresses.

"Here." She hands me the tissue. "It's almost time. I'm going to go check. You okay?"

"I'm great." I smile. "Started with a bullet, ended with a shotgun wedding."

She nods. "That pretty much sums it up, doesn't it?"

"I wouldn't have it any other way."

"That's my girl. Just one more look. Spin for me." She stares as I slowly turn. The dress has a beautiful lace overlay that covers my arms, and a bodice with a deep V in the front. The lace continues to the waist, and then a tulle skirt fills out the bottom with a modest flare. To me, it's like something out of a dream. I hope Lucius loves it as much as I do.

"Absolutely perfect." She beams. "Okay, I'm really going this time." She slips out of the white tent.

We're having the wedding at my family's property in a beautiful new gazebo Lucius had built. He even chose all the roses and flowers around it, making it a real-life dream. His wedding gift to me was the entire acreage. *"In case you need alone time. But you won't ever need alone time. And if you do, I'll just follow you over here until you realize alone time is overrated."*

I don't know how he's such a cinnamon bun to me

but death incarnate to our enemies. But he definitely pulls it off.

"Okay, we're on." Stella hurries around me, her emerald green dress a gorgeous look on her. "Let me do the veil." She reaches up and gently lays it over my face. "Perfect."

The string instruments start to play, and Stella rolls the girls in their cute little white double carriage out to strew the flower petals.

I wait, wondering if I made a mistake when I decided to go down the aisle on my own. I could've asked Sin or Teddy. I chose not to. Maybe because of Red, because I like to think the part of him that loved me—the good part of him—is still here. He wouldn't appreciate giving me away to Lucius, but I can't change who I love. That goes for both of them.

So, I'm going it alone. When I walk out there, I'll be greeting my family. Joining them. And I'll never walk alone again.

Taking a deep breath, I grab my bouquet of white hydrangea and pink peonies, then push out of the tent and start down the petal-strewn aisle.

When I look up, I almost lose my footing.

Lucius is absolutely gorgeous in a black tux, his smirk turning into a broad smile the moment he sees me. I keep walking, my heart pounding as I reach him beneath the gazebo.

"I've never seen anything so beautiful," he whispers in my ear.

I hand my bouquet to Stella and turn back to him.

When he reaches for my veil, his hands are steady as he lifts it. "There you are, my darling." He strokes my cheek, then takes my hands. His are warm and sure, his gaze never wavering.

Sin officiates, his voice carrying over the small group as the wind blows gently. I barely listen, my entire being focused on the man holding my hands—holding my heart.

When the ceremony is done and Lucius slides the ring on my finger, I feel like I might float away. And when he seals our vows with a kiss, I hold on tight. To him. To our life together. And to our future.

∽

If you haven't read the Acquisition Series, I suggest you begin with Sinclair, a FREE read.

If you'd like to read about another **Bad Guy**, check out Sebastian.

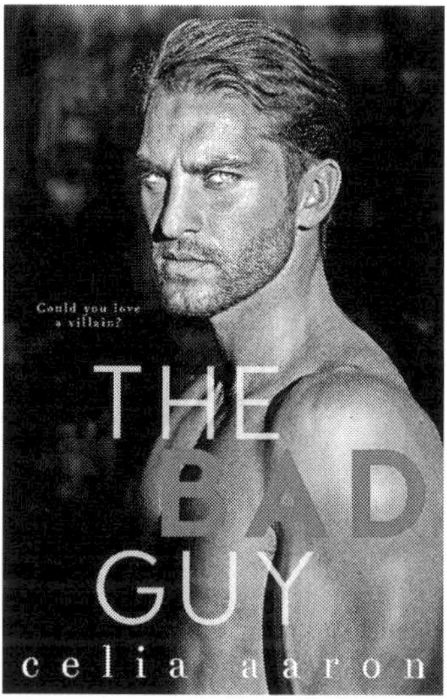
Could you love
a villain?
THE
BAD
GUY
celia aaron

ALSO BY CELIA AARON

Dark Romance

The Bad Guy

My name is Sebastian Lindstrom, and I'm the villain of this story.
I've decided to lay myself bare. To tell the truth for once in my hollow life, no matter how dark it gets. And I can assure you, it will get so dark that you'll find yourself feeling around the blackened corners of my mind, seeking a door handle that isn't there.
Don't mistake this for a confession. I neither seek forgiveness nor would I accept it. My sins are my own. They keep me company. Instead, this is the true tale of how I found her, how I stole her, and how I lost her. She was a damsel, one who already had her white

knight. But every fairy tale has a villain, someone waiting in the wings to rip it all down. A scoundrel who will set the world on fire if that means he gets what he wants. That's me.

I'm the bad guy.

The Cloister Series

I joined the Cloister to find the truth. But I've discovered so much more, and the darkness here is seducing me, pulling me down until all I can think of is him. Adam Monroe, the Prophet's son, a dark prince to an empire that grows by the day. He is tasked with keeping me safe from the wolves of the outside world. But the longer I stay at the Cloister, the more I realize the wolves are already inside and under the Prophet's control. If Adam discovers the real reason I'm here, he'll bay for my blood with the rest of them. Until then, I will be Delilah, an obedient servant of the Prophet during the day and Adam's Maiden at night.

Blackwood

I dig. It's what I do. I'll literally use a shovel to answer a question. Some answers, though, have been buried too deep for too long. But I'll find those, too. And I know where to dig—the Blackwood Estate on the edge of the Mississippi Delta. Garrett Blackwood is the only thing standing between me and the truth. A broken man—one with desires that dance in the darkest part of my soul—he's either my savior or my enemy. I'll dig until I find all his secrets. Then I'll run so he never finds mine. The only problem? He likes it when I run.

Dark Protector

From the moment I saw her through the window of her flower shop, something other than darkness took root inside me. Charlie shone like a beacon in a world that had long since lost any light. But she was never meant for me, a man that killed without remorse and collected bounties drenched in blood.
I thought staying away would keep her safe, would shield her from me. I was wrong. Danger followed in my wake like death at a slaughter house. I protected her from the threats that circled like black buzzards, kept her safe with kill after kill.
But everything comes with a price, especially second chances for a man like me.
Killing for her was easy. It was living for her that turned out to be the hard part.

Nate

I rescued Sabrina from a mafia bloodbath when she was 13. As the new head of the Philly syndicate, I sent

her to the best schools to keep her as far away from the life--and me--as possible. It worked perfectly. Until she turned 18. Until she came home. Until I realized that the timid girl was gone and in her place lived a smart mouth and a body that demanded my attention. I promised myself I'd resist her, for her own good.
I lied.

The Elder

In Azalea, Mississippi, the only thing hotter than the summer days are the men of the King family. When the patriarch Randall King is found dead, Detective Arabella Matthews will race the clock to stop the killer from striking again. Benton, the eldest of the King siblings, has to decide if he wants to cooperate with the feisty detective or conduct his own investigation. The more he finds out about his father--and the closer he gets to Arabella--the more he wants to keep her safe. But the killer has different plans . . .

Contemporary Romance

You've Got Fail

She's driving me crazy. Or am I the one driving myself

crazy? I can't tell anymore. Ever since Scarlet Rocket showed up in the flesh, she's turned my structured world upside down. My neatly ordered life, my hand-painted Aliens versus Vampires figurines, my expertly curated comics collection--none of these things provide any shelter from her sexy, sassy onslaught. It's a disaster of my own making. She didn't exist until I created her. Now, I can't get her out of my mind, and all I want to do is get her into my bed. Never mind that she's a thief, a liar, a con-woman. Every step she takes leaves chaos in her wake. And damn if I don't want more of it.

Kicked

Trent Carrington.
Trent Mr. Perfect-Has-Everyone-Fooled Carrington. He's the star quarterback, university scholar, and happens to be the sexiest man I've ever seen. He shines at any angle, and especially under the Saturday night stadium lights where I watch him from the sidelines. But I know the real him, the one who broke my heart and pretended I didn't exist for the past two years. I'm the third-string kicker, the only woman on the team and nothing better than a mascot. Until I'm not. Until I get my chance to earn a full scholarship and join the team as first-string. The only way I'll make the cut is to accept help from the one man I swore never to

trust again. The problem is, with each stolen glance and lingering touch, I begin to realize that trusting Trent isn't the problem. It's that I can't trust myself when I'm around him.

Tempting Eden

A modern re-telling of Jane Eyre that will leave you breathless...

Jack England

Eden Rochester is a force. A whirlwind of intensity and thinly-veiled passion. Over the past few years, I've worked hard to avoid my passions, to lock them up so they can't harm me—or anyone else—again. But Eden Rochester ignites every emotion I have. Every glance from her sharp eyes and each teasing word from her indulgent lips adds more fuel to the fire. Resisting her? Impossible. From the moment I held her in my arms, I had to have her. But tempting her into opening up could cost me my job and much, much more.

Eden Rochester

When Jack England crosses my path and knocks me off my high horse, something begins to shift. Imperceptible at first, the change grows each time he looks into my eyes or brushes against my skin. He's my assistant, but everything about him calls to me, tempts me. And once I give in, he shows me who he really is—dominant, passionate, and with a dark past. After long days of work and several hot nights, I realize the two of us are bound together. But my secrets won't stay buried, and they cut like a knife.

Bad Bitch

Bad Bitch Series, Book 1

They call me the Bad Bitch. A lesser woman might get her panties in a twist over it, but me? I'm the one who does the twisting. Whether it's in the courtroom or in the bedroom, I've never let anyone - much less a man - get the upper hand.
Except for that jerk attorney Lincoln Granade. He's dark, mysterious, smoking hot and sexy as hell. He's nothing but a bad, bad boy playing the part of an up and coming premiere attorney. I'm not worried about losing in a head to head battle with this guy. But he gets me all hot and bothered in a way no man has ever done before. I don't like a person being under my skin this much. It makes me want to let go of all control, makes me want to give in. This dangerous man makes me want to submit to him completely, again, and again, and again...

Hardass

Bad Bitch Series, Book 2

I cave in to no one. My hardass exterior is what makes

me one of the hottest defense lawyers around. It's why I'm the perfect guy to defend the notorious Bayou Butcher serial killer - and why I'll come out on top. Except this new associate I've hired is unnaturally skilled at putting chinks in my well-constructed armor. Her brazen talk and fiery attitude make me want to take control of her and silence her - in ways that will keep both of us busy till dawn. She drives me absolutely 100% crazy, but I need her for this case. I need her in my bed. I need her to let loose the man within me who fights with rage and loves with scorching desire...

Total Dick

Bad Bitch Series, Book 3

I'm your classic skirt chaser. A womanizer. A total d*ck. My reputation is dirtier than a New Orleans street after a Mardi Gras parade. I take unwinnable cases and win them. Where people see defeat, I see a big fat paycheck. And when most men see rejection, it's because the sexiest woman at the bar has already promised to go home with me.
But Scarlett Carmichael is the one person I can't seem to conquer. This too-cool former debutante has it all—class, attitude, and a body that begs to be worshiped. I've never worked with a person like her before—hell, I've never played nice with anyone before in my life,

and I'm not about to start with her. This woman wasn't meant to be played nicely with. It's going to be dirty. It's going to be hot. She's about to spend a lot of time with the biggest d*ck in town. And she's going to love every minute of it…

ABOUT THE AUTHOR

Celia Aaron is a recovering attorney who loves romance. Dark to light, angsty to funny, real to fantasy—if it's hot and strikes her fancy, she writes it. Thanks for reading.

Sign up for my newsletter at celiaaaron.com to get information on new releases. (I would never spam you or sell your info, just send you book news and goodies sometimes).

Newsletter Sign Up

Visit me:
www.celiaaaron.com